For the first time, there is something to be glad about in growing to five foot nine in ninth grade. I lift my bare feet on the pedals without resting my heels on the floor and feel the car's life through the clutch and gas and brake. It is so delicate and powerful, like Helen's dancing, like Daniel's guitar playing, like swimming in the dark, using all my senses to feel for the next movement and the next and the next.

Karen Romano Young

The Beetle and Me

A lOve Story

A Greenwillow Book
HarperTrophy®
An Imprint of HarperCollinsPublishers

Grateful acknowledgment is made to the following for permission to quote from copyright material:

From "Riding in My Car (Car Car Song)," Words and Music by Woody Guthrie, TRO—Copyright © 1954 (Renewed), 1969 (Renewed), Folkways Music Publishers, Inc., New York, NY. Used by Permission.

From *How to Keep Your Volkswagen Alive: A Manual of Step by Step Procedures for the Compleat Idiot*, John Muir Publications, Santa Fe, NM 87504.

Library of Congress Cataloging-in-Publication Data
Young, Karen Romano.
   The Beetle and me: a love story / by Karen Romano Young.
      p.   cm.
   "Greenwillow Books."
   Summary: Surrounded by her busy extended family and their many cars, fif-
teen-year-old Daisy pursues her goal of single-handedly restoring the car of her
dreams, the old purple Volkswagen Beetle from her childhood.
   ISBN 0-688-15922-2 — ISBN 0-380-73295-5 (pbk.)
   [1. Automobiles—Fiction.   2. Family life—Fiction.   3. Self-reliance—
Fiction.]   I. Title.
PZ7.Y8665Bg   1998   98-16327
[Fic]—dc21   CIP
                                                                          AC

First Harper Trophy edition, 2001
❖
Visit us on the World Wide Web!
www.harperchildrens.com

*For Dad, who taught me to keep my eyes
on the horizon
For Mom, who taught me how to get up
big hills in a little stick-shift car*

*And most of all for Mark,
who's been with me every inch of the way*

Acknowledgments

Thanks and love to those who read it first:
my sister Peggie; my cyberspace writers' group,
Debbie Keller and Debbie Duncan;
and especially my daughter Bethany.
And Dad, I thank you and your living,
breathing Porsche.

Contents

june   page 1

july   page 31

august   page 50

september   page 79

october   page 113

november   page 134

december   page 173

The Beetle and Me

june

This is the story of a car I had, a car I dreamed of having, a car I wanted even before I knew what kind of car I wanted, a car I started wondering about because my big sister, Helen, asked me what I'd drive if I could drive.

"So what kind of car do *you* want, Daisy?"

The story starts on the last day of school, when Helen and I are waiting for the bus. Cars are going by on Route 44: vans full of little kids; Chevys and Audis in shades of blue like business suits; the art teacher's Saab, mustard orange and shaped like a spaceship; red and yellow Beetles and Mustangs full of screaming seniors. Their windows flash spots of light. Their radios blare loud, foot-stomping, joyous summer music.

I watch, and think hard. A question about cars is a serious question in the Pandolfi family.

"Something different," I say finally.

Billy Hatcher, the auto shop teacher's pet, roars past in his black Thunderbird, and we watch after him jealously. Juniors with parking-lot privileges act sophisticated in rusty Datsuns and ratty old Novas and station wagons borrowed from their mothers. Next year Helen will be among them.

"How about a little Renault in dark green?"

"Nobody wants your slimy car, Helen."

"You're the one who said 'something different.'" She yawns, not even blinking at my mean words about the little old car that she paid for with every cent of baby-sitting or ballet-teaching money that she has ever earned since long before she turned sixteen.

Inside the bus Helen sits on her tailbone, graceful with her knees drawn up against the seat in front of her and her sundress tucked into the back of her knees. I sit behind her with my back against the window and my feet on the seat so that the seat of my shorts, not my bare legs, touches the sticky vinyl seat. I tuck my long red hair up into a knot, park it behind my head, and lean on it, feeling a welcome breeze come on my neck.

The bus grunts and groans and whines down the hill, spewing gray exhaust smoke through the open windows, and the moronic sophomore boys in the backseat begin to sing "Roll Out Those Lazy, Hazy, Crazy Days of Summer" at the top of their lungs. There is a lot of emphasis on the beer part.

Delicate Helen snorts and says, "A demonstration of remarkable maturity for boys of their ilk."

"Boys of their ick," I reply. "Where do they think they're going to get beer at their age?" Helen rolls her eyes at me. "It's findable, huh?" She nods and closes her eyes again. I look out the window at the trees in sun and shadow, and the cars, and wait for our stop.

Today I have no heavy textbooks, only my tattered, battered binder and the sweater I wore this morning in the cool. There is no homework, no final exam, no library trip scheduled for this afternoon. Summer vacation dawns on me and washes over me and stretches out before me like a road, empty and sunlit and ending invisibly among the trees.

I know exactly what I want to fill this summer with: I want a car.

"Hey, Daze." Helen's voice interrupts my thoughts. "Imogene and Ben are going to the lake to play ball and swim. Do you want to drive down and find them?"

This is awfully generous of Helen, who doesn't often wish to socialize with me and her friends together. It's probably just that her boyfriend, Bixby, has baseball practice this afternoon, and she doesn't want to be alone with Imogene and Ben. I wouldn't, either. All that show-offy hand-holding and whispering.

The bus winds down for our stop.

"Daisy?" Helen persists.

"No, thanks," I say, gathering up my stuff. "Too hot."

Helen shrugs, walks ahead of me down the steps.

The bus driver honks the horn. "Have a hot summer!"

Helen trots up the long driveway to get her bathing suit and baseball glove. I toss my book on the porch and walk to the top of the hill behind the battered red barn. I drop to the grass, go down on my side and roll, grass trees sky grass trees sky to the foot of the hill. The daylilies are beginning to sprout dark orange buds the same color as my hair.

I can dive and spin and climb without getting nervous or dizzy. Helen is the same. She can pirouette forty times without stopping, whipping her head around to spot the Nureyev poster on her bedroom wall every single time. And I can roll all the way down the meadow to the icehouse, stand up immediately, and not fall down. But today I need to think.

I lie there to give some thought to the matter of a car. It seems to me that I am the only one I know who has no car. I want a car. I need a car. No. I want a car that needs me. So what if I'm not old enough to drive? I'll get one. I'll have one.

My father has a car that is old, fast, and very lovely, a 1964 Porsche 356C in pale lemon yellow. He takes me along when he searches junkyards for the exact right hubcaps and bumpers and engine parts.

Over his desk in his office on the third floor of our old farmhouse my father has hung a photograph of my mother, standing beside his Porsche on a mountainy California road overlooking the Pacific Ocean.

My uncle Phil, Imogene's father, built his own car and races it on the weekends at the Lime Rock course. The first time I went to watch him race, when I was two, he won. His wife, Nicole, is a self-taught mechanic with her own garage. She runs his pit for him when he races, keeping track of tires and oil and screaming at anyone who makes one false move. (I should know.) Afterward she buys beers and sodas for everyone in the pit and serves chocolate chip cookies she makes herself.

What I want to drive is the same car I've always wanted: the purple Volkswagen Beetle we drove around in when I was a toddler only big enough to sit on Dad's lap and steer. I cried because I couldn't reach the pedals. Our old Beetle is dead, in storage down the meadow in the ancient icehouse. Now and again Dad robs it for parts, like robbing a grave.

I sit up among the lilies with buds dangling against my face and gaze out at the cars traveling Route 44. I wade through tall grass to get to the ice-house door. It is a square stone building, with two doors padlocked together. There is a small dark window-pane in the left-hand door. It reflects the sky and a bumblebee that has come along to bang himself against it. I wave the bee aside and feel for a milli-second the brush of fuzz plush against one finger. I can't see anything through the glass, just blackness, until I cup my hands around my eyes and shut out the light. Then there's one answering gleam from inside to tell me the Beetle's still there.

When you're a kid, the world opens up like a book that's already printed and unchangeable. You ask a question and your parents answer, and you believe whatever they say. But lately I want to ask my own questions and give my own answers. And what I tell myself right now is that I'm not sure Dad's Beetle is as dead as he says it is.

What could be worse than to be a car on your own in an icehouse, with nothing around you but darkness? We need each other, that car and I. I make a promise to myself then, and to the Beetle. It seems so simple to me, anything would on this last day of school first day of summer. I will make it go. I will make it my own.

An old truck tire hangs from the sugar maple in the yard, and after dinner I lie stomach down through the center of the tire. My arms dangle in front, my hair hangs in my eyes, and my bare feet turn me until the tire rope is twisted in a tight spiral. I pick up my feet, and the tire begins slowly to spin. My hair flies, and blonde Imogene and her three-year-old brother, Arny, and the orange cover of their book blur across my eyes. The rope straightens and begins to twist back on itself again, around and around and back, until I hang with my toes in the dirt, breathless.

"Do that to me, Daisy!" Arny pleads, dropping *Green Eggs and Ham* onto the back step.

Imogene says, "Aren't you a little old for that?"

"I'll quit doing it when I am," I tell her straight. They are my cousins, and they practically live here, although actually they have a house of their own (as I'm fond of telling Imogene) in town. I adore Arny, of course. He's easy and funny and sweet. But his sister! Imogene likes to make me feel young and silly and even more fifteen-year-old gawky than I really am. At sixteen (she was born just a month before Helen) she may as well have two or three years on me. She's blonde and pretty, while I'm orange-haired and not. She's round and curved where I'm bony and straight, although she's every bit as strong. She's loud, and she flirts, and she wears the kind of eye makeup Helen never would unless she were onstage. Today she's wearing blue mascara. Disgusting. Still, Helen and Imogene are as close, for our family, as my dad and Uncle Phil. "They're the ones who should be sisters," I said to Mom last week, but she answered just, "That *would* have made a difference." It didn't matter to me as much—their closeness—before my best friend, Katrin, moved to Pennsylvania.

Imogene: It pains me to think about her. But. We are cousins, and this family is our home, where we belong, so I guess I'd have to stick up for Imogene if it came to that—even if she can't spin on the tire without making herself sick. The fact is that we'd probably avoid each other completely if it weren't for Helen.

From upstairs we can hear Helen's off-key singing in the shower. Downstairs in the Friday-evening kitchen, Mom and Dad sit talking among paper plates and pizza boxes.

A red pickup truck catches Arny's eye as it turns into our driveway.

"Mom!" Arny shouts, jumping up. Imogene sits hugging the orange book to her chest, and waves as her parents pull up next to the barn.

Uncle Phil is my father's older brother. He has blond curls and brown eyes like my father, although his hair is now touched with white. He's tall and what he likes to call rangy. Aunt Nicole teases him and calls him mangy instead. Arny has his mother's brown hair, and brown eyes like both his parents. Only Imogene has blue eyes—true blue, not sea blue like mine, or the deep violet of Mom's and Helen's. As a group we don't look much like a family, we Pandolfis, but each of us resembles at least one other. Except for my eyes, I look like my mother; except for her eyes, Imogene is a female version of Uncle Phil.

Aunt Nicole bends forward and pulls the elastic band out of her ponytail, then shakes her long hair out, unzips her mechanic's coverall, and steps out, to reveal shorts and a T-shirt.

"You didn't warn me, girls!" she scolds us. "You didn't tell me it was going to get hot again!"

"Time to air-condition your garage, Mom." Imogene grins.

"Any day now, Imo," says Uncle Phil, kissing the top of her head and scooping up Arny for a hug.

"Did you eat?" asks Aunt Nicole.

"Yes," we answer, but Arny is ready for more and follows his mother inside. Uncle Phil grabs a slice of pizza from the kitchen and sits on the steps to eat it. Helen opens the screen door behind him and emerges scrubbed and dressed in shorts and sandals and a long embroidered blouse, ready for an evening at the lake.

"Who's the lucky guy, Miss Helen?" asks Uncle Phil.

"Who else?" I ask.

A long green station wagon has dropped some-one off at the end of our driveway. From my perch on the tire, I watch Helen watch Tom Bixby, his dark head and long body, as he makes his way up the hill to the house. Her eyes grow darker, the color in her cheeks gets higher, everything about her seems to deepen, as if the leaves on the trees had begun to glow because Bixby was walking beneath them.

When Bixby's not around, Helen has plenty to say about him—Tom this, Tom that—but when he arrives, she quiets. She sits still on the steps and waits for Bixby to get here, yet part of her seems to have gotten up and gone down the driveway to meet him.

"Hey," says Bixby, looking around at us all and adjusting his glasses.

"You coming down, Imogene?" Helen says.

"Not like this," Imogene answers, waving a hand toward the sweaty bandanna in her hair, her T-shirt and dusty shorts. "Now that Mom's here, I'll go home and take a shower. I'll come down with Ben in an hour."

"Okay," says Helen. "Ready?" she says to Tom.

"See you all," says Bixby, folding himself into the passenger seat of the Renault.

We wave as they drive off, and Uncle Phil comments, "She's got it bad."

"Why shouldn't she?" I ask, twirling slowly on the tire. I can never think of anything to say to Tom Bixby.

"Tall, dark, and handsome," says Imogene. "And he has the sense to wear red shirts."

"What?" Uncle Phil hoots.

"Did Helen go?" Mom pokes her red head out the door.

"Yes," says Uncle Phil. "And you should hear the review Bixby's getting."

"Oh. All that and brains, too?"

"Brains remains to be seen." It's true that Bixby hardly opens his mouth except to make some dumb joke.

"He sings nicely," Imogene puts in.

"Did you swim, Im?" calls Aunt Nicole.

"Yes. I'm going to steal the truck and go home for a shower, if it's all right. Ben and I are meeting Helen and Bixby."

"I'll swim!" Mom volunteers.

"Great," says Nicole.

"Me, too! I'll swim!" from Arny.

"Okay. What about you, Daisy?" Mom stands beside the tire and looks at me.

What about me? Should I go to the lake with the mothers and little Arny, sit there and watch Helen and Imogene and their pretty friends trying not to get thrown in the lake by their boyfriends, wondering what they'll be doing after it gets dark?

"No, thanks," I answer. "I'll stay here."

"Good," says Uncle Phil. "We're going to tune up the Porsche. A little extra manpower always helps."

"Especially if it's womanpower," comments Aunt Nicole.

The sun is setting behind our Berkshire hills when I take the pizza boxes outside and stack them behind the garbage cans. I sit on the porch steps, sipping iced tea mixed with lemonade. As the day-light fades, Dad and Uncle Phil turn on the barn lights. The doorway of the barn glows softly, casting orange beams onto the packed dirt and gravel of the driveway.

Inside the garage the yellow Porsche is parked in the place of honor under the work light, surrounded by tools and equipment and shelves full of objects that speak of my father's life, which consists, he says, of cars and women. Sounds glamorous, but the reality is spare tires beside pink-rimmed bicycle training wheels, plastic jugs of antifreeze along with bags of 5-10-5 fertilizer, neat sets of wrenches perched atop folded, deflated surf mats, and discarded Barbie lunch boxes full of spark plugs.

The Porsche's green canvas cover lies in a heap on the floor with Mom's brown striped cat, Ezekiel, curled on top. Under the hood my father and his brother put their heads together for a closer look at whatever's wrong with the engine this time. Nothing really is, but something can always be improved, made to run smoother or more efficiently.

One of the cars is always being worked on around here, and there are plenty to choose from. There's the Porsche and the car my father drives to his job as a computer programmer: a chocolate brown Saab, not spaceship-shaped but octagonal if you look at it from the end, one of the newer models, an '83, designed not to roll over, I think.

My mother drives a blue Mustang with a leaky convertible roof. If it pours rain, she gets Aunt Nicole to drop her off at the hospital in the pickup. Uncle Phil races a Class GTU white Mazda covered with STP logos. He drives a pale blue Chevy van to his job, teaching physics at the local branch of the state university. Imogene drives her red Honda Civic, even though she doesn't have the least idea what's under the hood. And now Helen has that Renault.

It might not seem that our family is lacking in cars, but to me there is one important car missing.

"Daisy?" calls my father. "Give us a hand here."

In the barn my father and uncle murmur and mutter to each other in the fix-that-car language they've evolved since Uncle Phil was sixteen and Dad was twelve. I set my iced-tea glass on the porch rail and pad into the garage on my bare feet.

"Behind the wheel, Daisy," says Dad, handing me his keys. I pick out the Porsche key with its red-and-black insignia and insert it in the ignition slot.

"No gas. Just start it." I turn the key and watch them looking with their ears cocked, glassy eyed as a couple of dogs listening for geese, as the engine turns over and begins its deep-voiced whir.

"A little gas now, Daisy," calls Uncle Phil, and I press the pedal lightly. He lifts his hand, palm up, and I press harder, watching his hand, until he holds it straight up. "Stop."

"Looks fine," says my father, gently dropping the hood. "Thanks, Daze."

Uncle Phil lifts Ezekiel off the tarp, and Dad and I raise it carefully over the Porsche. Uncle Phil hoists Ezekiel to his shoulder, scratches the cat's ears until he smiles and purrs.

"Home tonight, Daisy," Uncle Phil comments. "So what does this summer hold for you?"

"Oh, I don't know." I smile uncomfortably.

"No softball?"

"Daisy's sworn off organized sports," Dad

explains, giving the tarpaulin one last pat.

"Oh? How's your mother taking it?"

"She was all right about it," I answer. "I sat her down at the kitchen table and explained how I just couldn't stand it one more summer."

Uncle Phil laughs. "Good for you, hon."

"Uncle Phil?" I gather my nerve. "You were fifteen when you had your first car, weren't you?"

"That black Oldsmobile," he muses. "That's right. Why?"

"Well, where did you get it? Did you buy it yourself?"

"Newspaper money," he explains. "Almost five years' worth. And I spent every extra penny I had fixing it up."

"How much do you think a car like that would cost now?"

"An Olds?" He looks at me. "Or a fixer-upper?"

"Yes."

He looks at my father, who's listening with interest. "Couple hundred. Wouldn't you say, John?" My dad nods, raises one eyebrow.

Uncle Phil scrutinizes me. "How much have you got?"

"Four hundred seventy-five dollars," I say. I earn my money doing oil changes, and I'm a good saver.

"Good grief! Daisy, aren't you a little young for this?"

"How old were you, Dad?" He's standing there chewing on a blade of grass, and he smiles, with just one side of his mouth, and doesn't answer.

"He was eleven!" Uncle Phil sputters. "Eleven!

Followed me everywhere. Wouldn't let me out of his sight!"

"Too dangerous," says Dad, talking about the whole conversation, it seems. But he hasn't told me no. Wait until he hears which car I want.

"She's got a good head for it, you know, John. You ought to let her try."

At that Dad sighs. "I don't know, Daisy."

"The first Summer Cruise is tomorrow night at The Landing," Uncle Phil informs me. "Have a look at the wheels there."

I study my father's face. "Okay, Dad?" Maybe I'll have a better chance convincing Dad to let me buy a used car than to let me get the Beetle out of the icehouse.

"Okay, Daze. Come see what you see."

On summer Saturday nights my father and mother and Uncle Phil and Aunt Nicole and Arny go to the Summer Cruise, in town, at a drive-in hamburger place on the lakeshore called The Landing. It's a kind of car party where people can show off their cars and sometimes try to sell them.

Phil parks his van a few blocks out of town, on a quiet sunset street lined with tall, calm Victorian houses. We pile out and start walking.

You can hear the Cruise before you see it. A loudspeaker blares old music: Chuck Berry and Chubby Checker and "Leader of the Pack." Cars pull up all around The Landing. One by one, they fill the enormous parking lot. A man wearing a Hawaiian shirt announces each car's arrival as if it were a princess arriving at a ball, in between playing records and encouraging people to dance, eat hamburgers, and buy Summer Cruise T-shirts.

Cars are packed in everywhere at all angles, parked close together with just enough room between them for people to walk: a glowing black Model T with a little girl pumping the ooga horn; souped-up Chevys of enormous bulk, fat and wide and painted yellow with flames along the side, or airbrushed bubbles on a blue background; Buicks and Thunderbirds with big chrome-edged fins and dangerous-looking bumpers; a deep green Jaguar that slinks impossibly low, parked diagonally for extra space; little pickup trucks jacked up on gigantic wheels with names painted on: "Mister Sandman" and "Bad to the Bone."

Aunt Nicole snatches Mom's elbow. "Oooh, Melissa!"

She pulls Mom over to a big purple Buick with chubby red hearts and the name Passion Pit painted on the tail end. Inside, the backseat is folded down to reveal a bed, all made up in red satin sheets with a white satin quilted coverlet. The armrests hold bottles of champagne, and the windows have pull-down lavender shades with tassel pulls. Frank Sinatra murmurs on the stereo system, and red-and-white fuzzy dice complete the picture.

Mom and Aunt Nicole giggle over every detail, delighted and transfixed by it all. I leave them and walk off to look for Dad and Uncle Phil and Arny.

Instead I find the car of my dreams. It's a royal blue Volkswagen Beetle, with an oval rear window, parked under the spreading branches of an ancient sycamore tree. It's perfect. It's beautiful. And it's for sale.

I pull off a piece of sycamore bark and chew on it and stand there gazing spellbound at the black rubber, ribbed running board, the shiny chrome bumpers, the little VW insignias on the hubcaps and hood, the little sign in the window that says PLEASE DON'T TOUCH ME.

I know what damage oily fingers can do to a wax job, so I gently stroke the dry back of one finger along the dark fender.

"Watch it." A tall man with a gray ponytail emerges from the other side of the tree and approaches with a smile.

"I'm sorry!" I say. "I really do know better."

He laughs. "It's okay," he says. "I find it irresistible myself."

I turn back to the car. "It's old, isn't it?"

"Depends on what old means to you. It's a lot older than you are, young lady."

"1957," I answer.

His mouth drops a little. "How'd you know?"

"The back window," I say. "It's an oval. I was a baby in a 1957 Beetle." It was seventeen years old when I was born."

"So was my son," says the man. "But I doubt he'd know an oval from a split."

"I remember it so clearly," I tell him. "I always rode in the back in the well, with my sister. The carpeting was itchy on your legs in the summertime."

"Where is she now, that one?"

"In the icehouse in our meadow," I tell him ruefully. "I guess it's sort of a tomb."

"A tomb! Why? What's wrong with her?"

I shrug. "I don't know. No tires, for one. Rust? I don't know. We're all sort of scared of that place, us kids. I haven't spent all that much time looking around. I assume it's a dead"—I search for a word—"issue."

He studies my eyes and reads the lie. "A great man once said, 'It ain't over till it's over.'"

I chuckle. Helen has quoted the great man, Yogi Berra, to me many times.

"I'm sure my father would pronounce it dead."

"Your father? He's a coroner?"

"A mechanic."

"A mechanic with a Beetle like this on ice?"

He's got a point there. Still, I pride myself on being loyal. The only change I allow to register on my face is one raised eyebrow. He glances away awkwardly, but he's still smiling.

"So. Want to buy this one?"

Could it be that easy? "How much?"

"What can you offer?" He seems serious. I empty my whole bank account, all those oil changes.

"Four hundred seventy-five dollars."

He shakes his head slightly, and I back away a step. "I'm asking six thousand, bottom."

Naturally. How stupid can I be? This old car, in mint condition, with all its magic and charm? Of course it's worth thousands. Bottom.

Blushing horribly, I turn away and spy Arny, bouncing on my uncle's shoulder above the throng of people. As I go, the man with the perfect car calls after me.

"I'm sorry, dear. How old are you anyway?"

"Fifteen," I call back flatly, and shake tears back into the depths of my eyes.

Now the sky is completely dark, and stars have pricked through. I catch up with my family.

We walk along among the cars and reverently touch their gleaming sides, signs or no signs. I buy a strawberry milk shake and sip it, straw gurgling, as I look at Triumphs, Karmann Ghias, Porsches, Ferraris, and happy-looking classic Ford pickup trucks.

"What speed do you get in this baby?" Uncle Phil asks an old man with a red-and-black convertible Austin Healey.

The man smiles at his car tenderly. "Used to go drag racing with the honeybees," he muses. "Now we just buzz along."

Walking back to the car in the dark, between the glimmering fireflies, I think about what the man with the Austin Healey said. Speed doesn't matter to me, either. (I can't even drive yet.) I, too, want a car that I can liven up and keep alive with my hands, a car nobody else would think of wanting until they've seen what I've done for it.

My mother puts her arm around my shoulder. "See anything you like, honey?"

"They were all just beautiful, weren't they?" Aunt Nicole sighs.

I ask, "How much do you think those cars cost

when the people bought them?"

"That depends on whether they bought them new," Aunt Nicole answers. "Then it would be whatever the full price was at the time. Less if they were used."

"And what if it was a big mess and the person bought it to fix up?"

"Anywhere from a couple hundred dollars on up."

"Plus more money to fix it up," Mom adds.

"Right," says Dad. "It's a good investment if you know what you're doing. Those cars are worth thousands now."

"If you know what you're doing," Uncle Phil repeats wryly. "Those are key words." He shifts Arny from his shoulder to his hip. Arny's head is beginning to droop.

I feel stung. Doubly stung. "Can I carry Arny for you?" I ask. It feels good to put my arms around the heavy, warm little boy. In the next few blocks Arny's head drops on my shoulder as he falls asleep. At the car Aunt Nicole takes him from me and kisses his hair. As an afterthought she kisses me, too, on the top of my head, then looks into my face.

"Don't worry, Daisy," she says. "Maybe something will come rolling along."

I keep my bed pushed up right under the window so I can breathe the night air. Most of the time I like the feeling of being on the edge of outside, on the rim of the universe, but tonight it makes me a little nervous, as if things were out there in the shadowed woods beyond the meadow. Like the bug traps

Mom sets with holes in the vegetable garden, things wait for me to come along, stupid as a June bug, and fall in. I never do know what to say to people. I either say nothing or I say so much I get myself in trouble. It doesn't matter if it's people my own age or an old mechanic who only needs a tall, pointed hat to look like some great wizard of cars. Still, that car tonight made me remember all the restored Beetles I've seen at all the car shows I've been to, tagging along with Dad and Uncle Phil and Aunt Nicole. It can be done.

There is a knock at my door. "Come in," I call. It's Mom, with Ezekiel in her arms. She sits on my bed with her arm across me and looks up at the stars. Zeke snuggles in beside me, and I scratch his big old head between his ears.

"The Big Dipper," Mom says.

"Great Bear," I reply.

"Same stars," says Mom. To me it makes a difference: a bear rather than a spoon.

Mom lays her hand on my forehead and strokes back my hair. "You okay, Daze?"

"Hmm," I say, and turn to look out the window again.

"Did something happen to you at the Cruise?" she asks quietly. "You came back to us looking a little ruffled."

I place my hands over my face and peek out through my fingers. "I offered a man four hundred seventy-five dollars for a car," I say.

"And?"

"He was asking six thousand."

"Oops. But, Daisy, how were you supposed to know?"

I sigh. "I don't know. I just wish I had. I felt like such an idiot. He made me feel so young."

"Oh, dear heart! You *are* young." She reaches over and picks up, one by one, the framed photographs on my bedside table. Me with Arny at his christening. Mom and Dad in skis on the chairlift at Mohawk (taken by me from the chairlift in front of them). Helen and me at ages five and four. "What was it about this car that attracted you?"

"It was a blue Volkswagen like the one we had when we were little, except blue instead of purple. You know, Mom, the well, and the running board, and—"

"And the oval back window?"

Sometimes I think my mother makes a point of acting as if she knows nothing about cars so that now and then people in this family will talk about something else. But she knows a lot more than she lets on, a lot more than nothing. And she's tagged along at even more car shows than I have.

"Yes," I answer. "A '57."

She crosses her arms and fingers her elbows. "Well, Daisy, it could be worth that much if it was in good condition."

"That much!" I echo, and once more I feel the man's gentle, patronizing smile and my own tears of embarrassment. I flop back on the pillow and blink at the ceiling. "It was so great, Mom. I would love to do something like that. I would love to have our old one back again."

She studies me in the dim light. "Daisy, the engine on that car is decrepit. You realize that, don't you?"

When I don't answer, she goes on. "It was old when Dad bought it, you know. It went into the ice-house just before we went to California when you were five. Phil and Nicole and Imogene came and lived in the house while we were gone, you remember? I think Phil meant to lay a hand on it, but right about then his racing career began to pick up speed—you should pardon the expression, Daisy—and the Volks just went to pot. When we came back, it just didn't seem worth doing, and it still doesn't, my kid."

I am sitting up straight in bed. "So you're just going to leave it there rotting?"

"Not just me. We." She shrugs her shoulders. "These past ten years have been a busy, expensive time in our lives, Daisy, Don't get so upset."

"I want to see it!" What a picture I must make in my long T-shirt and socks and hair sticking out every which way, standing on the rug beside my bed, practically shrieking.

"Now?" Mom asks. "Daisy. Sweetheart, it's pitch-dark in there. You can have a look in the morning. But prepare yourself to be disappointed." She puts her hand on my shoulder and guides me back into bed as if I were a dazed little kid coming back from the bathroom in the middle of the night. She looks into my eyes and says, "That Beetle hasn't been run for years and years, and it might not run now. I'm not sure whether Daddy will want to get involved with it right now. I don't know whether you should, either."

"But it's there, right? So I can see it."

Mom sighs heavily. "Yeah, Daisy. You can see it tomorrow." She kisses me and goes out, shutting the door with a soft thud.

I sit up and rest my elbows on the windowsill and peer out to where the icehouse sits low among the green-silver waves of the meadow. It's not as if I've never seen the Beetle before. I've stood by and held nuts and flashlights while Dad removed parts to transplant them in other cars. I never gave a thought to whether there was anything alive in the Beetle. All I've seen up to now is that one secret gleam. Tomorrow, soon, I'll walk around it, tap it and touch it and even get under the hood. Somehow I know the Beetle is out there, in the pitch-dark of the icehouse, waiting for me.

Sunday I go downstairs at the crack of dawn, which is early this time of year, just two days past June 21, which Helen calls Midsummer Night, after a ballet she was in. It seems like Beginning of Summer to me, but that just shows how school gets in the way of nature, as if sitting in muggy class-rooms and riding heated buses on hot spring days haven't already gotten the point across. I've got a couple of hours before Mom hauls Helen and me off to church, which at least is air-conditioned.

The yellow Porsche has been pushed into the driveway between the house and the barn. Dad's idea of a Sunday-morning celebration is black coffee and work on the Porsche's valves. Today he has even bypassed the coffee in order to get to the car, so I put the old steel percolator on the stove. When it has perked its six minutes, I pour two mugs of black and take them out.

He's lying on his back under the car, wearing shorts, with his hairy legs and loafers sticking out. I remove a loafer and run a tickling fingernail up the sole of his foot, hear his head snap up and bang on a pipe. "Quit!" he growls.

"Coffee?" I offer.

"Yeah." He sounds pleased. "Got a ratchet out there, Daisy?"

I hand him one from the fold-up tool kit lying under the tree.

"Rag?"

I pass it over, feeling as if I'm assisting a surgeon. In a way I guess I am.

"Bitey wrench?" That the name Helen and I gave the adjustable wrench because of its movable jaw, which we used to screw onto each other's blue jeans bottoms, then run around screaming.

Dad slides out from under. "Coffee," he intones.

I sit with him on the rocky driveway, leaning against the warm red wood of the barn, letting silken dust run through my fingers, struggling to drink my coffee as black as Dad's. He sips continually, gabbing about what all needs doing under the Porsche, and I observe that he's finished half his coffee before I gather my nerve to speak.

"Dad?" I gulp finally. "It's about the Beetle you're keeping down in the icehouse?"

"Mmm?" He gets the gist right away, and his face takes on a very serious expression.

"Well. What are you doing with it?"

He shakes his head. "Not a single thing, Daisy. I haven't got the money to keep another car running, especially a car that needs as much as that one."

"I—"

"Oh, Daisy," he says gently, "that car needs a hell of a lot of work."

"I know," I say. "I—"

"Haven't we got enough cars around here that need maintenance? Do you think I have the time or energy to get that Bug out again?"

"I have, Dad. I could do it." I stare into his eyes to make him listen, and he studies me, his mouth wanting to say no.

"Based on what, Daisy? This car doesn't just need an oil change. It's got a rusted-through exhaust system. It's got an oil leak that's older than you are. It's tuned out and filthy in the bargain. You can't—"

"Couldn't I try? I'll spend my own money. I'll learn all I can. I'll listen to everyone's advice." I'm so worked up I hear myself making rash promises. "Dad, we can't just leave it down there."

"Aw, Daisy," Dad groans. "Don't go on about it."

I pick at a mosquito bite on my knee and fight the lump that's forming in my throat.

"I smell bacon, Daze. Let's go in."

I stand up stiffly and go inside to wash up.

Mom stands at the stove, laying strips of bacon on paper towels. "So!" she says brightly. "How's my old love bug?" I take it she means the Beetle, not Dad, and inside I feel a little bit hopeful.

"That's a dead issue, Melissa," says Dad severely. He reaches for the grease cleaner and scrubs his hands in the sink.

Mom glances at his face. "What's the big deal here, John?" she asks.

He turns angrily. "It's a big deal any time a fifteen-year-old girl thinks she knows more than a thirty-two-year-old car!"

"Not just any fifteen-year-old girl, John," Mom admonishes him. "Daisy's got a lot of thirty-eight-year-old talent bred in her. She knows a lot, and she'll know more once she attempts to restore this car."

"This car," repeats Dad. "Why this car?"

"Because it's the only car I could have!" I cry. "Even a car I *could* afford would cost so much money that by the time I was done paying for it, I wouldn't have money to fix it up."

He's silent, chewing a rasher of bacon. Mom scans his face, turns, and walks down the hall to the bathroom, walking out of the conversation.

I bring my eggs to the table and decide to press the point. "It's like when I was a little kid, and I saved up my money to buy a wallet like Mom's."

Dad smiles slightly. "Then you had nothing to put in the wallet, right?"

"Right."

"Nice wallet, but flat broke," Dad says. "Daisy, this is beside the point. Why does a fifteen-year-old girl need her own car?"

"Stop saying 'a fifteen-year-old girl,' John," Mom

tells him, returning. "It's Daisy, who happens to be fifteen. I was thinking." She pauses to assure his attention.

"On the john," states Dad.

Mom ignores this. "Just let Daisy see it. Let her decide if she wants to work on it, just work on it. She can't drive it anyway. She's too young for her own car, but she's not too young to learn mechanics."

Oh, well, Mom has missed the point entirely, but I see she's got her foot in Dad's door (maybe that *is* the point). He looks annoyed. He gets up and pours himself another cup of coffee, then turns toward the door.

"Come on, Daze," he says. The screen door bangs behind him, his loafers scuff the wooden steps, and he ambles off down the hill toward the icehouse.

My mother leans across the table on her elbows, with a little gleam in her eyes. "Move it, Daisy," she says lightly, and I bolt out the door and follow Dad.

The icehouse is dark, dank, dusty. Dad throws open the solid double doors, tossing daylight over the dim purple Volkswagen within. A tree limb bouncing in the morning breeze casts its shadow over the narrow windshield and makes the Beetle seem to blink in surprise. Dad rests both his arms on the roof tenderly and says, "Phil and I bought this car together, in high school. It was the first car I ever made go."

"Do you think it could go again?" I peer at his shadowed face.

My father rubs his shirtsleeve on the roof until a little shine begins to come. "Probably not."

Then what are we doing here? I can feel the Beetle waiting, hoping. I look at him carefully, at his hand on the roof turned palm up, cradling his coffee.

"You do so!" I say softly. "If you didn't, you wouldn't bother to protect the finish from your hot coffee."

Dad closes his eyes against me. "Reflex," he says.

He cracks the car door open, releases the emergency brake, and sets the gearshift in neutral. He moves his coffee to the dirt floor and sets his shoulder to the back of the car. I come and lean beside him.

"Push!"

Shadows of leaves and spatters of sunlight wash over the hood and roof and hatch. Then the Beetle stands in the bright daylight of the glossy green meadow.

"Marry a good mechanic." Uncle Phil grins when he sees the car.

"No, be one," says Aunt Nicole, lifting the hatch to examine the engine.

Uncle Phil chortles, bending his tall frame down to the little Volkswagen engine. "A very sick patient," he diagnoses. "Oh, ship of fools! Chariot of romance!"

"Really, Phil." Mom smiles. She and Helen stand shoulder to shoulder against the meadow wall, sizing things up.

"Why's Dad blushing?" Helen inquires.

With a groan, Dad answers, "I met your mother when I was driving this car. Like an elephant, my brother never forgets."

With her face to the sun, eyes closed (in embarrassment?), Mom says, "He asked me if I wanted to go flying. He said he was a pilot, and he wanted to show me the sky."

"No!" Helen laughs.

"Some line," Uncle Phil teases.

"She didn't know I was flying a Beetle," Dad says seriously.

"A different sort of adventure," Mom says to Aunt Nicole.

"Well, it did you in," Aunt Nicole counters.

"It wasn't the attitude, though."

"What then?" asks Helen.

"The altitude," suggests Uncle Phil.

"Oh, you know," Mom says airily. "Any guy who'd drive a purple VW . . . and those soft, velvety brown eyes . . ."

We all howl, and Uncle Phil says, "Just like a baby sea otter."

"Anyway. That's all ancient history," Mom announces.

Dad passes behind me to put his arm around Mom's shoulder and says, loud enough for all to hear, "So's this car."

I bend beside my uncle and look in at the dirty old engine. "Gunky and yuck" is my analysis. But I have one hand on the fender, so as not to offend it.

"Not as bad as it could be," Uncle Phil allows. And the force of all of us there together begins to wear Dad down.

"I've had it running now and then," he admits. "Just turned her over once in a while."

Mom raises her head and nods at him; she knew it all the time. "Good old love bug," she says softly.

Dad cups a hand under my chin and says, "Here's the deal, Daisy. I'll help where I can, but the grunt work is yours."

"What about money?" my practical mother asks.

"I have four hundred seventy-five dollars," I say.

"And an aunt who's in the business," says Uncle Phil.

"There are junkyards," Helen says. She'll never forget finding two perfect doors for her bashed-in Renault at the yard down in Danbury when she stopped on a whim one day on the way home from ballet.

"The whole thing ought to be in a junkyard," Dad says. He's kicking himself for keeping the Beetle around in the first place. "How are we even going to get it up to the barn?"

"We've both got big muscles," says saintly Helen.

"Please, Dad," I beg.

He's silent, staring at the old Beetle, before he turns and fixes me with serious brown eyes. "If I have other work to do, you'll have to be patient and wait. But if you can get it going, and keep it going, it's yours."

Helen leaps up and claps her hands together, just once before she is stopped by a look from Dad. My ears grow hot, and the hair on the back of my neck stands on end, and I'm smiling all over my face.

"Okay," I say.

"Start with a rag," says Dad, and I run joyfully for the shade and solitude of the big barn and the box of old undershirts nearly as old as my car.

july

Tom Bixby, Helen, Ben Van Buskirk, Imogene, and I lean our backs and shoulders into the Beetle and shove our legs hard against the damp grassy ground. With the driver's door open and his shoulder to the roof brace, Uncle Phil places the Beetle in neutral and gets ready to steer. Dad leans on the opposite side, shouting directions: "Watch the ditch! To the left! You, in the back, *mush*!"

Little by little the Beetle crawls away from the icehouse and up the hill to the barn. Arny, in the well behind the backseat, cheers and waves a little hand through the ajar back window.

In the yard we move to the front of the car and push her backward through the barn doorway to where Mom stands guiding us into the barn. At last we stand back, panting and sweaty.

The Beetle in the barn is a most satisfying sight, purple amid the brown shadows and spots of light, facing out the door of the big red barn. Over the door hangs a huge American flag, for the Fourth of July.

I feel like lighting fireworks, seeing my car there under the flag.

"Thank you," I say to the group at large.

Imogene and Ben flop on the kitchen steps, and Helen leans against Bixby's shoulder. Dad pulls sodas from the kitchen refrigerator and hands them out the door to Ben, who passes them around. Arny climbs on my old tricycle and pedals around the yard.

I have no social graces. That's what Imogene says. I can't dance; I can't flirt; I can't even talk to people, unless they're talking about cars or diving or driving or choir or something else I know about. Up to this year I've had only one real and true friend, Katrin Appleby, who moved to Pennsylvania in February, at the end of the swim-team season. At first we called, then we wrote, and now, well, I just think there's no looking back. It's not that I don't miss her, but I don't want to be the only one writing. Still, I begin to think there will be only one best friend in my life, and maybe Katrin was it. I miss her. I miss her! Katrin's absence would be a bigger problem this summer if I didn't have my car. But now there is a new problem: Helen.

On July 5 Tom Bixby and his family drive off in their camper to explore the Wild West, leaving Helen, as Dad puts it, unfit for human companionship. She spends the mornings in her room, stretching her leg muscles with her heel up on her dresser top, while with her hands she organizes her barrettes and fingernail polishes. With the door closed, she taps around the bare wood floor in her ballet shoes with their wooden toes, practicing pirouettes.

After eleven she haunts the mailbox. If a letter from Bixby doesn't come, she mopes and worries, "He's out roping cowgirls when it ought to be cows," even though she doesn't know whether Bixby is anywhere near a ranch. If she gets a letter, she cries, "He's so sweet, and I miss him so much!" Imogene, if she's there, makes strangling noises, and I pretend to faint from heartbreak, there in the driveway beside the mailbox, with a daylily clutched to my chest.

"Shut up," says Helen, laughing and crying, and kicks me as she passes.

"Hey!" I shout, and she retorts, noting the footprint she left on my leg, "You deserve to be dirty."

If there is softball practice, we are saved from Helen's relentlessly gloomy presence and from Imogene's merely annoying one. Then work actually gets done on the car. I am cleaning it part by part and, Helen says, I am gradually transferring the filth from the engine to my body.

"What exactly are you *doing*?" Imogene demands.

"I'm making a list."

"Making a mess, did you say?" says Dad.

"Checking it twice?" adds Uncle Phil.

"So who asked the peanut gallery?" Aunt Nicole inquires politely.

With the shop manual in one hand and a rag in the other, I'm trying to figure out what's missing, what needs replacement, and where I can find it all without spending too much of my money. I convince my father it's fair game to go halves on anything he robbed from the Beetle over the years, but he can't seem to make any deal without giving me the full history of whatever repair he did.

"I took the pulley nut out?" he'll answer in amazement when I accuse him. He'll stand there staring toward the Beetle, running his hand through his curly hair, and then admit, "Well, yes, I did. It was the day Helen had to get to tryouts for the traveling softball team. The Porsche was sounding a mite ragged. So I took a little run down to the icehouse. . . ."

Every time he owns up to a theft, he makes it sound as if it were Dad to the Rescue. He was getting me to church to sing in the children's choir at midnight mass on Christmas Eve. He was taking Helen, Imogene, Arny, and me to Kent Falls on the hottest day of the year. He was running errands, helping get Uncle Phil's Mazda ready for a qualifying heat at Lime Rock. It makes me feel funny, hearing these stories. Maybe they really were all rescue missions. Or maybe it's just that it's the first time I've thought of any of these events from Dad's point of view.

But it clues me in to something else, too. Dad still feels the Beetle is his car. And of course, it has been, up to now. When he thinks, he follows a kind of string of logic. All this listing of parts only leads him to remember who owns what. I will have to find a way of getting some distance between him and the Beetle. In Dad's view, being sixteen or having a license or enough money isn't what you need to drive a car—not any car of his anyway. You need to be able to get under the hood or down in the dirt and give it some serious medical rescue work. If I can just get him to let me do it, on my own, if he'll just give me some space . . . and in that space, I hope, I can do enough life-or-death work that what the Beetle becomes will be mine and mine alone.

One rainy afternoon when practice is canceled, Helen flops on her stomach across Mom's bed and watches her get ready for work. Mom works in the special-care nursery at the hospital, taking care of a few sick babies and a lot of premature ones, some of them terrifyingly small. She loves her work and tells us about many of the cases, even sometimes the ones who don't live. I'd never be brave enough to do what my mother does, and it's one of the things I love most about her.

Even on this moist day the nurse must wear white stockings, full slip, and a close-fitting polyester uniform. It's a day when Helen has had a letter from Bixby, gone off to cry in the barn, and returned to tell us that he's in Oregon, among the firs.

"How did you know you were in love?" Helen asks Mom. In my room next door I turn down the radio to listen.

"Oh," says Mom, taken aback. "Gracious. Well, I—"

"It was the car!" I yell obnoxiously, and sidle down the hall to stand in Mom's doorway.

"Daisy." Helen hushes me. "Tell me, Mom."

Mom brushes her hair out of her eyes, a little

shy. "I think it was a moment when I saw your dad looking at me with this look on his face, and I saw that he thought I was so beautiful. And I guess I realized how much I cared to have him think of me in that way. I'd never cared what anybody thought before, not anybody specific. And it meant a lot that he liked me just as I was at that moment. I loved him for that. Among other things. Guess I still do." She watches herself in the mirror, twisting her hair into a neat bun and securing it with hairpins.

"Where were you?" I ask.

"Out in the yard at home, getting the newspaper out of the mailbox. And your daddy came driving up—"

"See, it was the car."

"What were you wearing?" asks Helen.

Mom laughs, sets down her hairbrush, and turns to us. "That's the best part. My jeans, rolled up and full of sand from wading at the beach, one of my dad's old shirts, with the tail hanging out, and my red high-tops."

"Red high-top sneakers?" Helen is appalled.

"Yes." Mom smiles at us affectionately. "And I had feet as big as Daisy's."

"And style to match, from the sound of it," says Helen.

"Excuse me?" I pretend to be insulted.

"I've never had much style," Mom says unapologetically. This simply is not true. Mom has deep blue-violet eyes and looks beautiful even in her pajamas. "Why do you think I wanted a job where they tell me what to wear?" She turns to let me zip her stiff, white uniform back.

"So what happened?" Helen persists.

"Well. I was getting ready to go play softball. Instead I went drag racing with your father, and we won. I said it was the high-tops, but he said it was me."

She kneels down and pulls an ancient cardboard storage box from underneath her bed. Helen hitches herself on her stomach over to the edge of the bed and hangs over the box. Inside is Mom's wedding dress. We've seen that before, resplendent in its box, where it stays. Now Mom does something she's never done before. She lifts up the bottom of the dress and extracts an even more ancient pair of red high-top Converse basketball sneakers.

"Mom!" Helen sighs. "And you say you're not sentimental."

"This isn't sentimentality," Mom answers. "It's sentiment, a feeling, the real thing, you know? Daisy. Try them on?"

I sit on the rug and pull the sneakers on over my bare feet. They fit. For the first time in our lives Helen looks slightly envious of my big feet.

Mom pushes her own feet into her white nursing clogs.

"I've been waiting for you to grow up enough." I take it she doesn't mean size-wise. My feet have been size eleven since I was twelve.

"She's gruesome, all right," says jealous Helen.

I lace a sneaker up my ankle and tie the bow.

"Wear them then," Mom says. "May they bring you luck." She hesitates the slightest bit on the last word. Did she begin to say "love" and change it to "luck"? I'm much more ready for luck, and a purple Beetle, than love.

Helen makes her way through the streaming rain and finds me with my nose inside my car's engine, wiping and polishing and studying, taking apart the carburetor and putting it back together.

"Aren't you lovely," she comments, admiring my cut-off shorts, my big T-shirt tied in a knot, my hair also tied in a knot, and my bare feet.

"This is a weird car," she says when I don't respond. "Engine in the back instead of the front. Doesn't it have a radiator?"

I sigh. "Look for yourself, Helen."

"Well, don't get snooty about it." She looks for the radiator, doesn't find one, and laughs at herself. "Then what cools it?"

"Air," I answer. "It's called an air-cooled engine."

"Oh," says Helen blankly. "Ingenious."

"It is ingenious," I tell her. "The first Volkswagens were designed on commission from Hitler. They were supposed to be able to climb mountain roads without overheating, and they had to be priced so that workers could afford them."

"I suppose it was a success."

"Yes. So was Hitler, at first, you know. That was one of his good ideas."

Helen looks out at the rain thoughtfully. "They only teach you the bad ones in Twentieth-Century History. I'd say Volkswagens were a small contribution, in comparison to the bad he did."

"I know." I stop and look up at her.

"Where did you pick up all this information anyway?" Helen asks.

"The Porsche-Volkswagen Story."

"Naturally. Let me guess whose library that comes from." She opens the passenger door and sits on the seat with her legs out the door.

"Dad's gold mine." I wipe the crescent wrench on my shorts, causing Helen to wrinkle up her nose.

"Daisy? Do you really think the car helped them fall in love?" she asks.

"Maybe. A car can have its own magic. Look at how you feel about yours."

"Yeah," Helen allows, gazing out through the gray-green rain at her wet dark Renault. "Think it'll work for you?"

What is she talking about? The red high-tops?

"Go away," I tell her. But she stays.

"What are you going to do all summer, Daisy?" she asks.

"Just work on this car, I guess. It's what I want to do."

"All by yourself?"

"How else am I going to get the car for myself?"

"You could have just kept saving, like I did," she said. "Then Dad wouldn't even be part of it."

"I don't have the patience," I say. "I want it now. And I want *this* car, not any other."

She shakes her head. "You're a loony," she says. "What do you think he's going to do, sneak into the barn and do the work when you're not looking?"

"It's not that. I have to show I can do it myself."

"Show *who*?"

"All of them!" Dad. Uncle Phil. Aunt Nicole. Even her, the big sister, Helen.

She thinks for a moment, then stands up.

"Take a break?" she says. "Come down to the lake tomorrow with me and Imogene?"

"To swim?"

"No. At night." She's never asked me to do that before. If she goes at night, she goes with Bixby or Imogene.

"What are you going to do?" It's been forever since I've been diving at night, so I get very hopeful.

"Have a girls' night out. Bring the glow-in-the-dark Frisbee. Eat Popsicles."

"Cherry ones?"

"Whatever you want."

"Where's Ben?" There's something fishy about this.

"Well." She hesitates. "I don't know. I think Imogene's getting tired of him and his adoring gaze."

I can't imagine anyone at all gazing at me adoringly. I'm not sure I'd find it tiring.

"Okay." I rub my arm across my forehead, and the look on Helen's face tells me I've left a big grease mark there. "I'll come."

Helen is in the bathroom with the dimmer light on halfway, putting on her makeup in what she imagines will be evening light. I go in and sit sideways on the closed toilet lid, lean my back against the pink tile wall, and prop my feet on the sink.

"Comfortable?" Helen glances at me out of the corner of her eye. Faced straight ahead, she carefully applies foundation to her chin.

"Yeah. Got a cig?"

"You're a fool." Then, anxiously: "You're not smoking, are you, Daze?"

"Nah. Just being foolish." I examine my stubby fingernails. I keep them short so the engine grease doesn't show so much. "Helen. I know you can get a learner's permit at fifteen. What if you already know how to drive and can prove it? Can you get a license then?"

"Unh-unh. You still have to wait until you're sixteen to take the test."

Injustice. I drop my feet to the floor and sit up, gripping the edges of the toilet lid. I stare out into the outer space of my mind, where my Beetle, completely rebuilt and refurbished and shiny with Turtle Wax, sits at the edge of the driveway, without a driver. I see it moving down the road with Dad or Mom or Uncle Phil at the wheel.

"Boy, you're really putting yourself through it, aren't you?" Helen asks. I give her a dirty look. "Oh, quit sulking," she says, blush brush in hand. "Why is this a big deal, Daisy?"

I am silent, watching her brush blush over her cheeks and on the tip of her nose.

She goes on. "I mean, it's just the way it is. I didn't even get my permit until I was nearly sixteen because Mom didn't have time until summer, and Dad wouldn't take me."

"Why not?"

"Because I was the first one, that's why. Because I'm a girl."

"Is that what he said or what you say?" I ask. "That doesn't sound like Dad."

Helen tilts her head back and looks down her nose at her reflection, brushes mascara onto her eyelashes. In a steady, careful voice (not to jar her face), she says, "The real reason is he didn't want me on the road. He said he lost his license three times in his teens and he didn't want to watch me do the same thing."

This is thrilling information. How could he fix up the VW engine and fall in love with Mom with his license suspended half the time?

"But you're a good driver, Helen!" I protest.

"Because of Mom," she admits. "Because I waited for Mom to teach me, not that I had an option."

Well. This is all food for thought. Why is he letting me rebuild the car at all? How can you help an engine if you can't take it for a ride now and then, get things moving? Does he think I'm not going to get it done until I'm sixteen? What does he think I'm going to be doing until June 9 of next year? Does he want Mom to be the one to teach me to drive, in *his* Beetle?

"You're doing that thing Mom says, 'knitting your eyebrows together.'" Helen scrutinizes me closely, lipstick in one hand, mascara brush in the other. She's wearing a creamy white undershirt and pants and white ankle socks. She stands there in her underwear with her feet naturally turned out sideways in ballet first position, unselfconscious for once.

"You stand like a duck," I say.

She gives me a tired look. "What about some mascara, Daisy?"

It's my turn to act tired. "Oh, please don't."

"Come on. Just a little brown mascara. It would illuminate your eyes so beautifully."

This night at the lake with Helen and Imogene: maybe it's the beginning of something new in my life. If I'm old enough to have a car of my own, then maybe . . . "Must you?"

"Look down your nose. Now lift your chin. There." Ugh. Already I'm blinking too much. "Now, don't touch your eyes!"

"All night?"

She smiles at me, then chews her lip. "Is that what you're wearing, Daisy?"

I'm wearing dark pink jeans and a lavender T-shirt and the aquamarine Keds I bought at the drugstore. The Keds are the exact color of my eyes, sort of, which is a good reason to buy them unless you pause to think how often people see your feet and your eyes at the same moment. I hold my hands out to my sides and shrug. "Is that what you're wearing, Helen?"

"I just thought maybe you'd wear those high-tops."

"The colors don't go," I say, shrugging.

"Oh, get out of here, Daisy. I've made my mark on you for the night."

What she wears is brown jeans and a soft beige T-shirt, with a gold chain and gold earrings, and tan sandals on her small feet. Helen's feet are not beautiful, with their calluses and scars from ballet. Lovely

Imogene appears in a pale blue sundress, short, with mauve leggings and blue flat sandals. I haven't the foggiest notion what I'll look like in another year—or even two—but it's a fair bet I won't look like either of them. It's not something I waste a lot of energy worrying about.

On the grass lawn beside the lake Helen and Imogene and I toss the Frisbee around, back and forth. After a while two college-age boys in baseball shirts and shorts join in. They're good, able to catch behind their backs and to spin the Frisbee in such a way that it bounces off the ground and up so you can catch it. I guess I don't blame them for showing off.

The sun drops behind the trees, throwing long shadows with each leaf cast perfectly onto the sand. One of the boys aims the Frisbee at Imogene. She misses, laughing, and the Frisbee cartwheels along sideways into the shallow water behind me. Nobody watches where it goes. Imogene, hands on hips, says, "How could I catch a bullet like that?" and the boy who threw it shrugs, as if to say, "Oops, sorry, my amazing muscles got out of control for a minute."

Retrieving the Frisbee from the lake, I hear someone playing a guitar, picking soft bluesy rock like Jerry Lee Lewis would play at home alone, just for himself. I fling the Frisbee in the general direction of the muscleman, pick up my sneakers on two fingers, and wander off to find the guitar.

A boy with glasses and shaggy, blond-streaked tan hair is sitting on the concrete dock, cross-legged, playing a slow and moving version of "Flip Flop and

Fly." A good song for someone who's been playing Frisbee. I stand there stiff-legged, listening, and he plays on, ignoring me, and the sun gleams on his hair. He thumps the side of the guitar a few final beats and looks up at me. He has strong cheekbones and lines in his smile that are really long dimples in his cheeks. Crooked smile, but so appealing, and eyes of green-brown-gold—what color is that?

"What color would you say your eyes are?" I blurt.

He blinks at me, takes off his glasses, and peers at them as if he can see his eyes in them. Maybe I've embarrassed him.

"Mishmash," he answers. "Not green, not brown. My mother said hazel." A beautiful word, *hazel*, but it doesn't account for the gold flecks—or maybe the sunshine accounts for that.

He wipes his glasses on the tail of his blue shirt and puts them back on. "Yours are definitely blue," he tells me, "and you look like the sunset standing there." I'm not sure whether or not I am being complimented.

"Play some more?" I beg. Anything so I don't have to talk.

He gets off into Crosby, Stills, Nash and Young's "Suite: Judy Blue Eyes," with a look at me to see if I know it's called that. I open my mouth and start singing along on the dododododos and even harmonize a little, taking the high notes to contrast with his low tones. His voice is lovely, with warm tones and a range from 'way down south up to a falsetto. When we finish, someone on the beach actually claps.

He reaches across the guitar and shakes my hand. "I'm Daniel," he says.

"Daisy," I answer, and he smiles the way everyone always does when I give my name. Our hands are equally sweaty, his from playing the guitar, mine from nerves.

"That was some nice singing, Daisy," he says.

I wave the compliment away. "I listen to a lot of music," I tell him. He stomps into "Sittin' on the Dock of the Bay," and I sit there oh-so-comfortable, watching the dopey Frisbee fly and feeling my hair grow warm in the late sun.

"Stupid song," I say when he's done.

"There's a song for every occasion. What do you like to sing?"

"Any old thing," I say. At that moment the Frisbee whacks me in the back and Imogene comes trotting over.

"Daisy!" she says, so cheery. "What happened to you?"

I've fallen in love, I think to myself, but to Imogene I say, "My arm got tired, that's all."

"Not to mention the lure of irresistible guitar picking," interjects Daniel, smiling at Imogene. Boys always do.

"Daniel, this is my cousin Imogene," I say, looking behind her, "and my sister, Helen." The college muscle boys have tagged along, bringing a cooler of beer, and suddenly here we all are on the dock, this big group of people, with Daniel at the center. Not for a moment do I let myself think I'm anywhere near the center.

They pass bottles of beer around. I expect to be passed over, but instead a cold, hard bottle of beer materializes in my hand. Helen catches my eye, but one of the boys' faces appears to block my view. "Opener?" he says politely, and pops off the bottle cap with an attachment on his pocketknife. I have tasted sips from my mother's beer before, but it has never tasted the way this beer does on this July evening, bitter and bubbly, of earth and sunshine.

Imogene taps Daniel's arm, looks into his face, and requests, "Do you know any Simon and Garfunkel?"

He plays "Scarborough Fair," and I join in, singing the canticle, the high notes that dance over the top of the song in harmony. I've heard it plenty of times on Mom's old record. We watch each other's faces to get the rhythm right, and the others stop singing to listen. The sun has slid behind the earth, the sky above the lake is green, then lavender, then deep blue-purple, and suddenly above the edge of a hill peeks a peach-colored moon, ripe in the dark. Along the shore little Japanese lanterns are lit where someone's having a party, and the spotlight over the pavilion entrance has been turned on. In the glow I see Helen's eyes watching me, and the expression on her face is the oddest mixture of anxiety and surprise and tenderness: Where did I get this weird sister, and when did she learn to sing like this?

They all murmur appreciative words when we finish, and Imogene claps her hands. "Daisy, I had no idea!" she says with completely genuine good feeling. "One more Simon and Garfunkel song, please?" And he starts playing one I haven't heard.

I glance at Helen and see her watching Daniel intently, with her lips slightly open. If she were in her room alone, she'd be dancing to this one. I watch as Daniel looks at us all and then, catching Helen's look, settles his gaze on her face. He sings the rest of the song staring into her eyes. At the end she looks away, and shakes herself, and glances at me, then stares out over the lake where moored rowboats bob gently in the light breeze.

All of a sudden there's a lump in my throat and butterflies in my stomach. I wish I could just lean over backward into the water and swim away without anyone knowing I've gone. I can't disappear now, or Helen will know why, if she doesn't already. I can just imagine how blissful I looked when they first came to join Daniel and me on the dock. I set my face now, knowing that having no expression won't change Helen's—or Imogene's—assessment of the situation. I keep my mask on while Daniel and the gang wade through more soft folk songs. I drink another beer.

During "Puff the Magic Dragon" I tap Imogene's shoulder and say, "I'm going home," and wobble up the path, away from the lake.

Wide awake, and truly sober as a glass of water under my act, I walk home along the dark country road to Route 44. I figure I won't get home much before Helen, walking all four miles of it. To play it safe, I walk in the shadows. I'm not worried about criminals, not way out here. I don't want Helen to come along in her Renault, catch my bright clothes in her headlights and slow down. I don't want her to know I've left because some guy I've never seen before whom suddenly I'd die for would rather look at her than me. I don't want her to think I've left for any other reason than to go play glow-in-the-dark Frisbee on the big lawn or gaze at the summer moon and stars.

I'll go home to my Beetle, I tell myself. A car is what I wanted this summer, not luck or love or anything else, and I've got it, and I'm reviving it just as well as Aunt Nicole or Dad or that man with the blue Beetle at the Summer Cruise. I hug this thought against me and keep it there all the long way home.

august

In the muggy dusk of an early August day, I prop Arny on my hip and inch between the shiny maroon and green sides of a pair of Packards. It's another Summer Cruise, and I'm looking for a certain blue Volkswagen Beetle. I remember it dreamlike, and I wonder if the effect will be the same after four weeks of working on my purple car.

In contrast with the dimness of my Beetle's outer shell, the blue one looks even more heavenly, something to look forward to at the end of the long road of repairs that lies before me this summer. Beside it sits something from another dream: Daniel, with his guitar slung across his back. The ponytail man is there, too, talking to Daniel. Both of them turn toward me with a smile.

"Daisy!" Daniel holds out a welcoming hand. "You and my father have met?"

"In a manner of speaking," the man says. "I'm Dennis Schweitzer. I didn't know you were a friend of Daniel's."

"We just met once," I say, looking at Daniel, and the butterflies commence fluttering in my stomach. "I'm Daisy Pandolfi, and this is Arny."

"You have a brother, too?" Daniel asks.

"My cousin. He's Imogene's brother. You remember Imogene?"

"Sure."

After this burst of talk Daniel and I find ourselves with nothing to say.

"So," Mr. Schweitzer says. "Still in the market for a Volksie, Daisy?"

"No, actually," I'm pleased to say. "I'm restoring my father's old one, the '57 I told you about." I set Arny on his feet in front of me.

"Ah!"

"It's the same as yours, remember? Oval window."

"And you're really doing it!" Mr. Schweitzer extends a big hand toward Daniel. "You know, when Daniel was as big as Arny here, he used to be my copilot." He opens the passenger door and rummages in the glove compartment, comes up with a black-and-white photograph of a curly-headed boy about Arny's size, big eyed and grinning in the well at the back of the car.

"Aw, Dad." Daniel pretends embarrassment. He kneels down beside me to show the picture to Arny. "That was me," Daniel tells Arny.

"That was me, too," I say, and he looks up at me with a smile.

"And Helen, I suppose."

"I guess so."

"Where are the ladies tonight?" asks Daniel.

"They have a softball game."

"In the dark?"

"There are big lights."

"So, Arny," says Mr. Schweitzer, "what do you drive?"

"A race car," Arny answers.

I laugh. "Sometimes you do, huh, Arny?" I explain, "His father races Class GTU Mazdas."

"Who would that be?"

"His name's Phil Pandolfi."

Mr. Schweitzer shakes his head. "We don't know too many people around here yet, do we, Daniel? Just moved here from Boston in the spring." He pauses, then goes on, "Where do they race?"

"All over. The next one's at Lime Rock, in a couple of weeks."

"Good luck to him. And Daisy, listen. These VWs have a few tricks up their sleeves. I want you to let me know if you need any kind of help." Mr. Schweitzer's eyes are direct; his voice is kind and sincere. "Let Daniel know. He'll get a message to me." He walks off to find a soda.

"Tell me about the high school." Daniel pulls his guitar to his front, strums a few chords. "Are there plays? Theater groups? Choirs?"

"Oh, yes," I respond. "There's a musical in fall, a drama in spring, and Cabaret Theater. There are all kinds of choruses, one for each year, and a concert choir."

"Great." Daniel sighs. "That's good. Does Helen sing?"

"No, but Imogene and I do. She's in concert choir, and she's usually in the chorus of the musicals."

Daniel nods. "Poor Helen," he says. "Can't she sing?" He doesn't seem too interested in Imogene.

"Not at all. She dances, though."

"In the musicals?" He brightens at the suggestion.

"Not so far. She does ballet, jazz. They have their own recitals."

"And Daisy?"

"I sing. I made concert choir this year," I report proudly.

"You should. I've heard you sing." We smile at each other, remembering, and I jump to my feet.

"Better go, Arny." I kneel and pick up my cousin, piggyback style.

"Good luck with your Bug," calls Daniel. "I'd like to see it one day."

"Okay!" My silly heart is hammering. Why not stay and talk? Why should just thinking about that night at the lake shoot me to my feet as though I'd sat on a bee?

On a hot morning a week later when steam rises from the meadow, Dad and Uncle Phil and I push the Beetle out of the barn into the yard so we can have a good look at the engine in the light. Dad gives me a demonstration of how to replace a spark plug, then stands over me criticizing and encouraging as I do one on my own. Finally Dad trusts me enough to walk away and do some job or other at his workbench, but Uncle Phil lingers close.

"Your dad and I had a look at this engine last night," he says after a while. It looks as though Dad has put him up to talking to me, even though he's perfectly capable of butting in on his niece's life without any encouragement from Dad.

I cock my head in a listening way, not trusting myself to make a polite response.

"I haven't changed my initial assessment."

"Huh?"

"My, uh, preliminary diagnosis."

I turn to look at him. "English, please," I say. It's not like Uncle Phil to be so vague.

"It's a very sick patient, Daisy. Even if you get it all tuned up, it's a bomb waiting to go off." Excuse me. Did I say he was vague? I take it back.

"What are you, Phil, the voice of doom?"

"*Uncle* Phil," says Dad from his dark corner.

"Daisy, babe, you're surrounded by years and years of experience," says Uncle Phil.

I stand up straight and face both of them, bracing my back against the shoulder of my car. "You guys didn't have any experience when you were starting out." Is that as dumb as it sounds? I don't know, but somehow they seem to take my point.

Uncle Phil says, as if Dad weren't there, "John wasn't ever going to do anything with that VW."

"Phil—" Dad begins, but I say across his words, "You mean it's no big loss?"

Uncle Phil shrugs and glances at Dad, who turns away toward his workbench again.

"Well, it would be a loss to me," I say firmly,

feeling my brows draw together, tense and intense.

"That's what we're afraid of," says Dad.

We. Them. And me on the outside, apart. "That's how I want it," I say.

And we all seem to agree it's enough discussion for one day. They start welding the bumper on the van, and their noise shuts down the talk.

I'm up to my wrists in my engine when I feel a tap on my shoulder. It's Daniel. Behind him in the driveway stands a little yellow motorbike.

"I looked you up in the phone book," he says. "I thought I'd come by and see your Beetle."

"Well," I say, "ta-da." It looks fine, if I say so myself, dusty purple in the bright sunshine. "Just needs a few adjustments."

"Yeah." Daniel snorts. "More than a few, I'd say. Is it doable?"

"Of course."

"Is it worth it?" There is no answer to that.

"Time will tell," says Dad over Daniel's shoulder. Guess he's learned to hear around welding noise. Dad's got his back up; who is this kid to ask whether or not a car of his is worth it?

Daniel, with his hands in the pockets of his jeans, surveys the barnyard, the vegetable garden, the house, whistles—what's that tune?—"Home Sweet Home."

"Pretty place, Daisy," he says sincerely. "You should have horses, or cows, or something." Uncle Phil looks at me with his eyes crossed, and I have to look away.

"Cars." I grin. I remember my manners all of a

sudden and introduce him to Dad and Uncle Phil. "Want a drink?" As we escape from the barn, I see the Pandolfi brothers exchange a very fishy look.

In the kitchen I scrub my hands and pour us a glass of iced tea and lemonade. My Beetle sits splendidly in the yard with its hood yawning, a purple work in progress.

Helen runs thumping down the stairs and through the kitchen and almost tramples Daniel and me as we sit on the steps.

"Hi!" she says in surprise.

Daniel gives her a warm smile and reaches out to shake her hand. Ill at ease with his formality, Helen extends her hand and he takes it.

"Delighted!" he says gallantly. All of a sudden I feel like I'm the one who barged in on the conversation, instead of Helen.

"I'm paying a Beetle visit," Daniel explains.

"Well," says Helen brightly, "it's not a live Beetle yet, but at least it's only half dead." I give her a kick.

"Brat, Daisy." She grins. "We'll be done playing ball at two. Come down on your bike and have a swim?"

Suddenly all the corners of my life are coming together at one intersection. Cars. Family. Swimming. And now Daniel.

"Maybe," I say. Anything could happen.

"See you," says Helen. We watch her trot across to her Renault and drive away. Only Helen could look lovely on her way to play softball—or on the way home, for that matter. Red shorts, Bixby's baseball shirt with BIXBY in square black letters that span his broad shoulders but wrinkle on Helen's, black cleats, and her hair in one braid tied with a blue rubber band.

"Your sister's very beautiful," Daniel tells me.

This is not news. "Thank you," I respond, oh so graciously.

"Who's Bixby?"

"Her true love."

"Oh?" Very nonchalantly. "Where is he?"

"He's traveling the back roads of America."

"Huh. Good for him."

Daniel watches the back of Helen's car as it disappears down Route 44. He turns and glares around the yard and fixes his eyes on my car.

"You ought to put some wax on that," says Daniel. "A little elbow grease would have her looking gorgeous in no time."

"I'll get the engine working first," I say. "It's been sitting idle for so many years. It needs so much: engine grease, not elbow grease."

"Sure, but a little shine would improve your outlook. Let me show you."

He goes into the barn and asks Dad for some Turtle Wax, comes back with a can and a little rag. I don't want to picture Dad's face.

"You know," I say, "I know how to do that." I reach for the can, but he snatches it away.

"Ah, but you don't know when to do it," Daniel says. "A little polish will give it sex appeal, motivate you for the dirty work that must be done." He sings, very cornily, "This little car of mine, I'm gonna make it shine." I'm tickled and smile at his sparkling eyes (hazel) and spy Uncle Phil watching me with a mixture of dismay and amusement as I dig into those spark plugs and Daniel goes to work on the fender. In about five minutes it's a perfect arc of deep purple-gold-green gleaming magic. I straighten up to have a look, and see my face beside Daniel's, reflected slightly lavender.

"You get the idea," he says. He drops his waxy rag on top of the car and rubs his hands clean on another. "If you'd like, Daisy, I'll come by around two and ride you down to the lake."

"Okay," I answer. "I'll have to ask, but I'm sure it'll be all right."

"Maybe your cousin would like to come along?" asks Daniel. I thought it was Helen he had a yen for.

"She'll be there," I say. "She plays softball with Helen."

"Good." He goes off on his motorbike, and Uncle Phil looks up and waves.

"Nice enough guy," says Uncle Phil.

Dad unbends himself from his welding and walks out of the barn to the driveway. "Nice-looking fender," comments Dad. "How many spark plugs have you gotten done, Daisy?"

"One," I answer meekly, and stick my head back in the engine.

At the lake there is a bunch of us: Helen and Imogene, and a few girls from the softball team, and Daniel and me. Ben and some of his friends show up with a loud radio and a case of beer. Everyone gets introduced to Daniel, who blends in gracefully and makes a point of talking to everyone. Gone are the moments alone this morning. I admire the reddish gleams in his blond hair and his smooth tan shoulders. I remind myself of the way his back felt under my hands as I held on to him on the motorbike: warm and hard and oddly familiar. I remind myself that I brought him here, that he's here because of me. So what if all he knows about cars is Turtle Wax?

It's easy to get along with people when you're swimming because you don't really have to do or say anything. You can swim along quietly, among everybody, and feel like part of things. Imogene is up on the float on the diving board, showing off, horsing around, lovely and bright in a silvery green bathing suit, doing cannonballs and Li'l Abners with the boys.

"Diving contest!" she calls. "Helen! Daisy! Get up here!" Ever since we've been able to swim, Helen and Imogene and I have held diving contests. Every summer, in this very lake, we make it a point to learn one new dive. Last year it was backward somersaults. I haul myself up the ladder and onto the float, wishing for a little more flesh on my bathing suit–covered bones. At least I can dive, which is more than Imogene can do, most days.

"All right!" Helen announces. "This year's challenge: front somersaults." Uh-oh. They are harder than backward somersaults, but Helen manages to do one, a little lopsided, on her first try.

It's my turn, and I flip but land flat on my back, *wham*, smacking the surface of the water.

"Next time, jump a little higher," says Daniel. He

gets up to take his turn, and I sigh to myself, watching him: We have diving in common, too.

Then it's the big show-off's turn.

"Here goes!" Imogene yells with aplomb. She gets lucky, and executes a perfect front somersault, then catches her right foot with a bang on the diving board as she comes down. She emerges from the water white faced and swims back to the beach to check the damage. She sits on the sandy shore, cradling her foot, which shows an ugly purple bruise and is beginning to swell. Helen and I follow her in. The others stand on the float, watching.

"Is it broken?" I ask, sitting in the water. "Do you want some ice?"

Helen takes Imogene's foot gently in her lap and feels for a break. "Can you move it?"

Imogene wiggles her ankle around obediently.

"No," Helen says. "A bad bruise, though, Imo."

"Oh." Imogene sighs in relief. "Play-offs are in another month."

Helen nods. "You'd better stay off it awhile, though."

"You all right, Im?" Ben wades in, with Daniel and the others trailing behind.

"Yeah. I just want to go home now, I think." She looks appealingly at Helen.

"I don't have Mom's car today," says Ben regretfully.

"I'll ride you on the bike," Daniel volunteers.

"I can take you," says Helen. "Daisy, will you get our stuff?"

Imogene stops me. "No," she says. She extends

her hand to Daniel, just like that, right in front of Ben, and he pulls her to her feet. "Daisy has hardly gone swimming all summer. You two stay. I'll go with Daniel." She pulls on her shirt and shorts and goes hobbling alongside Daniel up the path to the parking lot where the yellow motorbike is waiting. Nobody looks at Ben or me.

Helen sits on her towel and looks out at the lake, shading her eyes with her hand. "Is this all right with you, Daisy?"

I turn toward her, but she's looking the other way. I shrug my shoulders. "It'll have to be," I answer. I clench my teeth to keep my chin from wobbling.

One thing about Helen: She never makes me talk about anything. But she cusses and blows off steam about the injustice to Ben all the way home. What makes it all the worse is the way Ben sat and talked to me after Imogene and Daniel left, sitting on the edge of the sand while both of us pretended not to be thinking of the little motorbike buzzing off up Route 44. Ben asked me about the car he'd heard I was fixing up, and he suggested I take auto shop in the fall. ("There's nothing Mr. Fitz doesn't know about cars.") Way too nice for Imogene. And I think that if Ben weren't talking to me, he would have gone in the woods to cry.

Eventually Helen stood up and wrapped her towel around her waist and said she was supposed to be at ballet by five. Ben's friend Billy Hatcher, who'd been sitting quietly on a towel while Ben talked to me, came along and stalked on long, skinny legs up the path to his black Thunderbird waiting in the parking lot.

We all said a big cheerful, noisy (fake) good-bye, and we drove home.

And now there is Mom, in the kitchen with Arny, who is here because Aunt Nicole had to take Imogene for an X ray. One look from Mom tells me she has read the story of this whole sorry afternoon in my face. That's all it takes to send me bolting out to the barn.

I grab a long-necked light and swing it over my car's engine. I know it so well now, after just a month of taking care of it, and I love the smooth hard metal under my hand. Don't cry, I tell myself. Just look at what you've done with this car. Shiny fat cams. Plain gray crankcase. Rocker arms like a row of silver see-saws. I imagine my Beetle flying along Route 44, gleaming with a coat of wax from bumper to bright bumper, not just on one faded fender.

There's a hand on my shoulder, and I spin around, thinking, Daniel!

"Take it easy," says the gravelly voice. "It's just your old dad."

"When can I drive this thing?" I burst out angrily, almost whining. "Isn't it about time I learned to shift gears for myself?"

But Dad can't be shaken off that easily. He gives my shoulder a tender rub. "Soon," he says. "I went over the job you did on the spark plugs." I bristle at that, and he holds up one finger to hush me. "If you do that well on your points, you'll be on the road in the next few—"

I spin out from under his hand. "You went over it?" I ask. "You're not supposed to go *over* it. I'm the one who owns the grunt work."

"And you're doing it." Dad's eyes are intent on my face. "Don't get too far ahead of yourself, Daisy." His voice tells me he's heard all I have to say on the subject, and there's no use arguing. Dad bows out and begins picking through his Porsche shop manual for something.

I get to work on the points, not caring about my wet bathing suit or the towel I dropped on the dirt floor. He'll see. So will Aunt Nicole and Uncle Phil and Daniel and Ben and all of them. When I start my engine up, it'll purr, it'll sing, it'll buzz as sweetly as any cute little yellow motorbike.

But there's something else that has to happen to my Beetle first, before it can fly. To accomplish it, I'll have to face Daniel Schweitzer again.

Mr. Schweitzer's blue Beetle is parked under the sycamore tree as usual. He's nowhere to be seen, but there is a guitar case in the backseat. And there's Daniel, in a black T-shirt and jeans, softly strumming his guitar in the grass. I stare for a moment, the back of my neck prickly hot. Is it the car that draws me here, or him?

"Hi," I say uncertainly. "I was hoping to find your father here."

"Not tonight. Tonight I'm car-sitting."

"Still for sale?"

"Eternally. I'm not sure he'd ever really sell it, though."

"Then why show it?"

"For the oohs and aahs."

"Well, it gets plenty of those." I sigh. "It's so pretty."

"You really think so, don't you?" Daniel says lightly.

"Sure. I'd have bought it in a moment if only I'd had the money."

"He'd have just upped the price."

Now my entire face is hot. "Then why do you have to show it?"

"Oh, I don't know, Daisy." Daniel strikes a few angry chords. "You can get somewhere with a car. Where can you get with a guitar?"

I study the top of his head. "I see," I say. "A car is sensible. It can take you places. Where's a guitar going to take you?"

He doesn't answer, so I go on. "Strange and wonderful places."

He nods. "Yes. But those places are all inside my head. They're outside of here and now." He imitates his father, "'A car increases its value in time. Old songs are just old songs.'"

"No," I protest. "A car increases its value, but you only see that increase if you sell it!"

Daniel looks at me with new appreciation, his eyes more gold than green in the glow of the floodlights. "And the old songs?"

"They get better with time. You don't get tired of the good ones."

Daniel looks away, listening to "Peggy Sue," the old song blaring over the loudspeaker. "Anyway, you wanted my father for something?"

"I need to see how he does a valve job."

"A what?"

"Valves. The little doors that open and close in the cylinder heads. You know."

"No, I don't know. Or maybe I just refuse to know."

"All right then, mine need adjustment."

"Watch it, Daisy." Daniel raises a warning finger. "You're becoming one with your vehicle. It's not advisable."

I've heard this line before from Imogene. "My car," I correct myself, and smile to hide the little pang his words give me.

"So you were wondering, since you and dear old Dad have the same model," he says in a slightly sarcastic voice, "could he give you a little demo of this . . . valve . . . thing?"

He's making me embarrassed.

"I'll ask him for you." Abruptly.

"Thanks." I stand up and brush grass off my jeans. "I'd better see if I can find my uncle."

"Why? Need a ride?"

"Yes."

"I'll drive you. This place is winding down anyway. It gets cold these late August nights."

He packs up his guitar, and I get in the car and inhale. It's wonderful, vinyl and leather, and full of ancient history. Daniel starts it up, and it sounds wonderful, too, as if it's been running forever, not one part out of harmony.

"This is what my car would be like if it had been

babied all these years," I say.

"I take it yours hasn't?"

"No," I say regretfully.

"It will be," Daniel says kindly. He drives well, treats the car gently and respectfully.

He turns on the radio and we sing along with the Talking Heads song they're playing. That's a relief, since we don't seem to know what to say to each other when we're not singing or talking car. If only I weren't so tongue-tied. If only he were more interested in cars. If only . . .

Just the kitchen is lit. Nobody home yet.

"I'll give you my number," Daniel says, "so you can call my father." He leans over the back of the seat and opens his guitar case, pulls out a sheet of scored music paper, and writes.

"Thanks for the ride," I say, letting myself out.

"Good night, Daisy."

I go inside and up to bed. I stand the piece of paper against my clock on the bedside table and lie looking out at the sky until I fall asleep.

Sunday morning my bedroom door creaks open, and Helen creeps in. She gets into bed with me, taking most of the covers. "I'm supposed to tell you to get up for church," she says.

"When did you get home?" I ask.

"Before midnight, like a good girl." She rolls onto her stomach and props herself up on her elbows. "Only just, though. Imogene spent the whole evening running away from Ben."

She looks at me with her eyebrows raised. I'm

sure my face shows my disgust. She changes the subject. "You, Daisy, you sneak, what did you do last night?"

"Went to the Cruise. You know. You dropped me off."

"And?" She pokes me in the side. "How did you get home? Aunt Nicole said they never saw you."

"Daniel Schweitzer was there. He gave me a ride in his father's car."

"That Volkswagen? So I suspected! You innocently promised me you'd find Phil and Nicole, but instead you went home with handsome, talented Daniel Schweitzer."

"He's not handsome." I protest the silly-sounding word. "Anyway, Hel, it's you he likes. Every time I see him he looks around to see if you're there, and his face falls when you're not." And yet I think of how he smiled when I sang along with the car radio, and hope springs a little. Oh, face it, Daisy, hope springs a lot.

"Daisy girl. You'd better watch it. You should see your face when you talk about him."

"I can't help it. He's not interested, though. He doesn't even like that car, that beautiful car! He positively sneers about it. If only he did, we'd have so much in common—"

"Yeah? What would you do, go racing?"

"At least we'd have something to talk about."

"You're in luck," says Mr. Schweitzer. "I've got an engine on blocks in the garage."

"Great." That was fast, I think. Didn't I just see

that car at the Cruise last Saturday night?

"It's his spare engine, Daisy," Daniel explains.

"Oh," I say stupidly.

"I bought it at a VW fair last spring," Mr. Schweitzer tells me. "I'm rebuilding it."

"Then he's going to put it in the car and rebuild the old one," says Daniel. "It's his hobby."

I smile, but Daniel's father doesn't.

"Of course all this will make it easier to see the valves work," he says. He walks into the garage.

"Coming?" I ask Daniel.

He gives me a look. "I wouldn't miss it."

"You know," I whisper, "I think my father wishes he had a son."

"So does mine," answers Daniel.

"Come on." I challenge him, leading the way to the garage, with Daniel tagging behind.

"All right, Daisy." Mr. Schweitzer beckons me. "Show me my cylinder heads."

"There, and there." I point out the two big metal loaves of bread on either side of the gleaming crankcase.

"Where are my valves?"

I indicate the valve covers on each side.

"Go ahead," he says.

The engine is clean enough for me to take off the valve covers with bare hands, exposing well-oiled valve springs and rocker arms beneath.

"Now, Daniel," says Mr. Schweitzer, "hand me the big wrench." Daniel picks up a large crescent wrench, and I wince.

"The socket wrench, please," Mr. Schweitzer

says patiently. He bends to adjust the big nut at the end of the generator, and Daniel gives me a see-what-I-mean? look. I shrug, then watch Daniel's eyes glaze over as Mr. Schweitzer explains how to get to "top dead center" for each cylinder. Although I'm sympathetic toward Daniel, I need to know about this, so I tune in.

"Next, find the wrench that fits the nuts on top of the valve, and get used to how to loosen up."

Well, I'm used to playing surgical assistant to my father while he works on his car, so I automatically pick out the right side wrench.

"Very nice!" Mr. Schweitzer smiles for the first time since I arrived, as if maybe this won't be a chore after all.

To be fair, I explain, "My father drives a 1964 Porsche. It's almost the same engine. I thought it might be the same nut."

"Okay."

We both look up, realizing at the same time that Daniel has left us. I hear stereo music begin in another part of the house. I feel a little pang of hurt for Daniel. This mechanics stuff isn't that difficult once you've got a reason to be interested. But, as Imogene tells me, if you're not interested, you're not interested.

I watch Mr. Schweitzer adjust his number-one cylinder exhaust valve to 0.006 inch, using a feeler gauge to get it just right, so it moves just a tiny motion. He does the same with the intake valve. Then he has me turn the big wrench 180 degrees, to top dead center for cylinder two. I instruct him through the second pair of valves and do the third and fourth sets myself.

"Fine." Mr. Schweitzer pats my shoulder. "You'll be a good one, Daisy."

"I suppose it'll be a different thing from underneath the car," I say.

He chuckles. "Yes, but you've got the feel of it now. Listen, I've got to get to work on a rack for this spare engine. Just bang on Daniel's door and ask him to drive you home."

"Thank you," I say.

"Let me know if you have any trouble. We're always at The Landing Saturday nights. Just Cruise down."

At the racetrack at Lime Rock a few drivers are out early, taking practice runs. Their wheels steam and hiss amid puddles of last night's rain. Their engines whine like mosquitoes, their cars disappear around the curve as effortlessly as marbles in a maze. Their driving is so smooth that the cars seem to roll, never accelerating or braking, moved by invisible force.

I see them in my mind's eye through the barn window where I stand picking through the tools on Dad's workbench.

"Hey, Daze." My father stands in the barn doorway beside the Beetle, silhouetted against the morning light. "What are you after?"

"Uh." I stare back. "Feeler gauge."

He walks toward me, and his face emerging from the shadows is anxious. "You're doing those valves this morning?"

I look away down the workbench to the envelope Dad left on the Beetle's front seat three days ago, his vote of confidence: the registration for the Beetle, updated. He doesn't sound so confident now.

"I thought I'd better." A light, cool breeze through the window brings up goose bumps along my arms, and I shiver.

"Won't be summer long," says Dad. "Why not play another day and come watch your unk?"

"School starts next week, Dad," I explain. "I want to have it all going nice and smooth by then. I'm going to have so much homework and stuff I'll only have time for maintenance."

My father fingers the sockets in the wrench case, turning them over and fitting them into their slots. His chin on his chest, he looks at me sidelong. "You know what you're doing with those valves?"

"I do."

"Never showed you that on the Beetle. Did Nick—"

"No," I mutter, "Mr. Schweitzer gave me a demonstration on his."

Silence. He picks over the sockets some more, then turns and takes my chin in his hand. "When I said you owned the grunt work, I also said I'd help. Why didn't you ask me?"

"Dad. You could have shown me the valves on the Porsche, but it's all backward. Mr. Schweitzer could show me them on the same engine as I have, and he even had one up on blocks."

He nods. "It's different on your back under the car, sweetie."

"I know, but I've watched Aunt Nicole and you do that."

"Tell you what, wait till Tuesday night. I'll come home and give you a hand."

Biting my lip, I shake my head. "I want to do it myself."

"Want me to look it over afterward?"

I hesitate. It would be best to be sure. Silently I shake my head.

"A car can live or die based on valve adjustment, Daisy."

I nod. He sighs. Then at last he grins and hugs me. "All right! All right! Your valves. Your car!"

"Look at it this way, Dad. You've been teaching me all my life. I'm going to use it now."

"You talk a good story."

The screen door slams, and Mom calls, "John!"

"Coming," he calls. Then: "Listen, babe, that Bixby kid is coming home today. You leave Helen alone, okay?"

"Of course I will!" I am stung by the insinuation that I wouldn't. I guess last summer I was still doing a lot of tagging along, Katrin and I, teasing and driving Helen and Imogene crazy. But not now. This summer she has invited me along.

Dad winces. "Of course you will. Aw, Daisy, can't I tell you anything anymore?"

I shrug, rubbing the goose bumps on my forearms.

"You're growing up so fast," Dad says.

"Not fast enough," I answer, all my uncertainty filling those three words and making them shake.

He chuckles. "Yeah, I guess you would think that." He kisses my cheek.

"Tell Uncle Phil safe ride, okay?"

"I'll tell him."

I'm under my car on my back in the driveway, rags beside me, wrench and screwdriver on my stomach, and the feeler gauge in my hand.

Carefully I insert the feeler gauge in the exhaust valve of cylinder one and loosen the nut on the rocker arm. I drop the wrench and pick up the screwdriver to undo the screw. Tighten the nut. Insert the gauge again. Too tight now. Loosen the nut and the screw. Tighten the nuts. Check the gauge *again*. I try to remember how Mr. Schweitzer's valve felt, on the block in his garage. He's right, Dad's right, Aunt Nicole's right: It's hard to tell what I'm doing, upside down and flat on my back, with my arm wedged inside the engine.

If the car could talk, it would be asking a lot of nervous questions, like a patient going into surgery. "I'm doing my best," I tell it aloud. I want a second opinion, says the car.

Someone kicks my foot. "Daisy?"

It's Helen. "Huh?"

"I'm going to pick up Bixby now." How she's trying to sound casual!

"Oh, baby, baby," I tease.

"Good luck with your valve action, fool!" she says, laughing.

Poor Helen! She sounds nervous. I hear her car start up and drive away. On my back, not so cold anymore, I check my exhaust valve one more time to see if the gauge slides in just right. What was Helen doing when she was fifteen? Certainly not messing around under any cars. No, Helen had already had a few dates: bowling with a boy from summer camp, movies with kids from school, and parties I never got the full details of, no matter how much she and Imogene giggled and whispered.

No, here I am, moving along to the intake valve now, adjust that nut, screw that screw, jiggle the gauge, pop out from underneath and rotate the engine, back under with wrench and screwdriver and feeler, and so on until, no longer cold, no longer comfortable, dripping sweat, I move through all four cylinders. This is me at fifteen, this is Daisy, mooning over a boy a year older than I am who's clearly interested in my cousin or my sister—one of them, if not both, and not me at all—and mooning over a car I won't be able to drive for at least ten more months.

The phone rings on the barn wall, and I jump from the depths of concentration back to the real space around me so fast that I bang my head on the Beetle's bumper. Uncle Phil!

I grab the phone. "Hello?" Tell me it's all right!

A voice comes to me as though down a long glass hallway. "Daisy?" It's Mom, sounding very everyday-ish.

"You made me jump! I thought Uncle Phil—"

"No. If you're so panicked, why aren't you here? Or is that why?"

But I can't tell Mom that Uncle Phil is the one and only race-car driver who could never crash and die. For me, that's absolutely true. But the cars around me would argue, they are so heavy and real, dark and fast and dangerous. "No," I say. "I'm nervous because I'm doing my valve job."

"So John said." She usually calls Dad "your father." "I didn't let him tell Nicole that you were attempting such a thing." John. Nicole. She makes them sound like kids at school, just human beings. Is that what they are? You mean, things could go wrong—for them, for me, for my Beetle?

"Mom," I say, "I'm not going to explain what I'm doing to every single person in this family." I'm waving the bitey wrench above my head, more dramatic on the phone than I'd ever dare to be if she were standing here in the barn with me. "I'm . . . doing . . . my . . . own . . . valve . . . job!" I separate each word to make it clear and definite. Girl mechanic goes berserk—and not a soul here to witness my courage.

But Mom remains calm. "Why, Daisy?"

"Why?"

"Yes, why?"

"Just because," I yell into the phone.

In the background then I hear Imogene's voice: Imogene, the good daughter who's there to cheer her father on; Imogene, the cute blue-eyed girl who forcefully grabbed the cute hazel-eyed Daniel, who's not tortured by nonworking cars.

When at last I finish the eighth valve and haul myself out onto the driveway, it's early afternoon. Helen's car is back, though I never heard it come. So where are they, Helen and Bixby? There they are, at the other end of the meadow, sitting on the stone wall, talking, watching the cars go by, light brown hair and dark brown hair blowing in the breeze. I was going to start up my engine, but now I think I won't make any noise.

I bend to the side mirror and examine my face, smeared with dirt and grease, wiry red hair pulled back in a dusty braid. For no special reason I feel like crying, with prickly eyes and a lump in my throat. I go inside, run upstairs to my room, dump my clothes on the floor, and jump in the shower, to wash the whole day away.

There comes an evening when I let the Beetle's hood down gently and Dad looks up and says, "Let's take her for a ride." I feel light infuse my face. He smiles at the blush, opens the door, and hands me into the driver's seat.

I turn the key in the ignition and tap the gas, feel the engine spark and turn over, and rev it, and at long last hear that Volkswagen engine giggle and sing, like jingle bells inside a rubber ball. As I've seen Dad do, I shift to first, and take my foot slowly off the clutch. Too fast! The car lurches into the doorway and stalls. We sit with our back end in the darkness of the barn, our faces turned to the meadow light, for all the world like some animal half born.

I glance at Dad's face. "Sure you want me to do this?"

He's silent for a long moment. "Tell me something, Daisy," he says at last. "Do you intend to keep growing older?"

"Nothing I can do to stop it, is there?"

"Exactly," he says bleakly, and while I'm puzzling over this, he points to my thick-soled, red high-tops. "Take your shoes off."

All right. The car needs a driver. I am too young to have any right or reason to drive this car, but who has more right, more reason, than I? And I'm getting older, sitting here hesitating.

My bare foot presses down on my car's clutch pedal. Calmly, I tell the car. Gently, it says back. It's not the first time I've ever engaged a clutch, but it's the first time I've done it because I was about to drive somewhere.

"Now let up, until you feel it catch," my father directs.

"Catch what?"

"Mmm, let up till it thickens, till you feel it's ready. Just do it and you'll see. You'll feel. Have your right foot ready to give it a little gas when the clutch takes."

I learn to drive my car on the rutted dirt road behind our house, the road that curves up from the river, from down in the gully at the bottom where the river actually flows across the road in the spring. I let out the clutch and give it gas until the gears mesh, shifting slowly through second to third among the summer cabins and tall woods until the road flattens and the Beetle flies, riding flat out, across the hilltop between the fields of corn and cows.

I learn to drive because I must drive my car, because Dad knows I must, but I know I can't really drive it anywhere, legally, until I'm sixteen. The car is ready now, so I drive it now and wonder what will happen to us both before I turn sixteen next June.

For the first time, there is something to be glad about in growing to five foot nine in ninth grade. I lift my bare feet on the pedals without resting my heels on the floor and feel the car's life through the clutch and gas and brake. It is so delicate and powerful, like Helen's dancing, like Daniel's guitar playing, like swimming in the dark, using all my senses to feel for the next movement and the next and the next.

september

I'm a sophomore. I think that sounds good until Imogene tells me it means "fool." I can tell she's planning to spend the year saying I'm sophomoric. I would never have thought I'd catch myself saying this, but thank God for school. Here I am, walking down the hall in my red high-tops. I'm a new person. I've got my own car. I'm ready for anything. Most of all, I'm ready to look at something besides the underside of a Volkswagen. I'm ready to listen to something besides Helen talking on the phone with Bixby, in the living room with Bixby, in the yard with Bixby. And I'm ready to think about something other than whether my valve job will hold, and if so, for how long?

I can't help feeling that I've gotten away with something and that my days of being proud of my Beetle's easy hum are numbered.

"Please, Mrs. Muir"—I'm in the guidance office at school, begging—"I have to take auto shop. If I could just talk to Mr. Fitz about it?"

I have caught Mrs. Muir at just the right moment: rushed and exasperated. She pushes at her gray curls and regards me steadily. "Go right ahead, my dear. Talk to Mr. Fitz." She hands me my schedule briskly. "If he approves, have him write me a note. I must warn you, though, be prepared for disappointment."

"Thanks, Mrs. Muir. Thanks!"

Light on my mother's lucky sneakers, I trot along the main hallway past the auditorium, down a little stairway to the dimly lit hall that leads to the auto shop. Learning what I need to know to rebuild my car has begun to seem like a series of obstacles to melt, break, evade, and puncture. "Be prepared for disappointment." Never! In my good-luck red hightops and my blue jeans, my big white sweatshirt with the Y for Yale on it (when Uncle Phil sees it, he always says, "Y not?"), I stride into the shop, hoping I look confident.

At the doorway to the shop I pause. I've been in Aunt Nicole's garage so many times, and it has always seemed a lot like this: smelly, gray, noisy, orderly, greasy, and bright, an adult place where I was welcomed as a child. This is an adult place where I must be an adult, yet I've already been told that I'm too young. Too young, maybe, but still desperate and shameless.

Sticking out from under a big American engine are two black high-top sneakers. I give one a little nudge with my foot, and Ben's friend Billy Hatcher emerges.

"What?" he asks simply, looking up at me from the floor.

"Is Mr. Fitz here?" Billy stands up, shoves back his dark brown hair, and looks around. He is tall and thin and plain-looking, bony in that strung-together way some boys have.

"I don't see him. Do you? He must have gone down to the teachers' room for coffee. He does that sometimes."

"And what do you do?"

He shrugs, indicates the oil-stained coverall that drapes his long frame. "I carry on. What do you need?" Then he says, "You're the one with the Volkswagen, aren't you?" He says Volks-*wagon*, like the thing Arny pulls around his backyard. It kind of makes my ears jump. The bell rings and saves me from answering, and the hall begins to vibrate from many footsteps upstairs.

People begin to appear, including Ben, who pulls me to a seat beside him. "You got in!"

I hush him. "Not yet."

Mr. Fitz lurches into the classroom. He's tall and loose-limbed, with smoothly combed, straight white hair. His intimidating appearance shakes me.

"Gentlemen!" he begins, and, looking around, adds, "and ladies." Thank goodness there's another girl, a senior, sitting at the front.

Mr. Fitz calls the roll, fifteen names, only one of which belongs to a girl, Jean Reade. I listen as they all answer, "Here," in their turn, and I imagine that as a boy my age Mr. Fitz must have been every bit as tall as he is now, but thin and gangly like Billy Hatcher, with big feet and hands, his hair shorn in a crew cut or some other old-timey style. Thinking this helps me calm the nervousness in my stomach.

"And your name, miss?" Mr. Fitz addresses me, pencil poised.

"Daisy Pandolfi," I answer, waiting for the smirk, but Mr. Fitz's face does not change.

"Year?"

"Sophomore." Fool. Mr. Fitz lays down his pencil.

"This is an upperclassman elective," he says kindly. "I'm afraid you are not eligible."

"My guidance counselor said if I get your permission, I can take the class."

"In that case, I'm going to have to ask you to leave, Miss—"

"Pandolfi. Daisy. Please, Mr. Fitz. I need to learn mechanics."

He folds his arms across his chest, checks his watch, stone faced.

"And what do you drive, young lady?" His tone tells me that he's been very patient with me, but my time is running out.

"A 1957 Volkswagen Beetle."

He cocks his head. "You drive this car?"

My neck grows hot. "On back roads," I answer. "With my father."

"I assume you know you're not old enough to drive without a license?"

I take a deep breath. "Yes, Mr. Fitz. I'll be sixteen next June. Until then I want to keep my engine running."

"She's restored it herself, Mr. Fitz," Ben interjects. "She's done nothing but work on that engine all summer." Some of the faces around me look interested.

Clearly Mr. Fitz would like to move on, out of this discussion.

"Give her a try, Mr. Fitz." Billy speaks up. Mr. Fitz shoots Billy a look of irritation. "I bet most of the people in this class haven't rebuilt an engine." Something tells me Billy is one of them.

"I have to stay until the bell anyway," I say hastily. "Underclassmen can't leave early."

"Stay till the bell then," says Mr. Fitz dismissively.

I breathe out slowly and give a little grateful smile to Ben and to Billy Hatcher, who shrugs one shoulder and looks away.

Mr. Fitz calls us over to a big engine on blocks at one side of the class. "Miss Pandolfi." He challenges me. "Since you're an expert on the VW, tell us three differences between this engine and your car's."

"My engine is in the back of the car," I say. "This one would be in the front."

His mouth twitches, as if to say, Can't you do better than that?

"The VW has no radiator. It's air cooled."

Mr. Fitz shows some interest. "And this car? What cools this engine?"

"The water."

"Go on."

I press a fingertip on a cam near the top of the engine and take a deep breath. "My Beetle has a push-rod, rocker-actuated valve train," I say. "This engine has cams over the cylinder head."

"Making it . . . ?" Mr. Fitz glares around at the class, daring them to answer.

"An overhead cam engine," I finish.

"What's the difference?"

"An overhead cam is supposed to be more efficient," says Jean.

"Why?" Mr. Fitz points an accusing finger at Ben, who looks blank.

"All right!" says Mr. Fitz. "This is where we start." He herds us back to our seats and begins a lecture on the phases of an engine.

At the bell I carry my schedule up to Mr. Fitz and lay it on his lectern before him. Without looking at me, he signs it, then hands it to me.

"Keep your nose clean, Daisy," he tells me. His eyes are nearly as pale green as Ezekiel's.

All those pirouettes Helen practiced while waiting for Bixby all summer must have paid off because she got the part of the Sugarplum Fairy in *The Nutcracker*. I've decided I won't be on the diving team this fall. It's too lonesome without Helen and my friend Katrin. If Daniel were willing to put his diving talents to good use—but no, every time I see him he's gabbing with Miss Ferguson about the fall musical, about Cabaret Theater in the winter, and every other drama or musical event that might be in the wind.

Daniel goes around school with his guitar in a cloth bag across his back, and his hair so long and soft and shaggy. He's like no one this school has ever seen before. I can't help it: My eyes follow him wherever he goes. And I'm not the only one.

Upperclassmen have parking privileges, but more often than not Imogene leaves her Honda home and catches a lift with Helen and me as we swing through town in the morning on the way to school. Every day but Friday I take the bus home because Helen leaves straight from school for her ballet rehearsal in New Haven. I stand there waiting for the bus and observe how Imogene gets home. For the first few days I see her walking. And then suddenly every day she's on the back of a certain yellow motorbike, with the guitar slung across her shoulders since she's in the back.

Helen drives me home from school on Friday. On the way we stop at Imogene's, for no real reason, just to hang around, Helen says. With softball finished for the season—their team lost by one run in the first round of the state tournament—Helen and Imogene don't know what to do with themselves at night. Helen seems particularly lost on Friday afternoons and nights when Bixby has soccer practice.

"You need a new sport," I tell Helen, dropping into a deep leather chair in Imogene's living room. Phil and Nicole's house is different from ours, which has its own special brand of sloppy comfort. Here there are pale green rugs and a lot of flat Scandinavian furniture, set off with abstract pastel paintings in shapes like paper cutouts, and punctuated with Arny's yellow Tonka trucks.

Imogene tosses me a can of soda. "A new sport?" she repeats. "I do, too. Somehow I can't cope with the idea of basketball." She waggles her ankle, which held up just fine through softball.

"It's all in your head," I tell her.

"Well, naturally she'd be nervous," says Helen, with a glance at me.

"Diving star Daisy *doesn't* see," says Imogene. "Don't you realize, Daisy? My life flashed before my eyes!"

"And what did you see?" I ask.

"Static." Imogene grins.

"Uh-huh," says Helen acidly.

"I'm going to try something completely new," says Imogene, still stuck on the subject of herself. "If you're going to do ballet all winter, why shouldn't I try something beside strict athletics?"

Helen looks blank. "Like what?"

"Well, we're juniors now. It's important to look well rounded."

Helen snorts. "Keep putting away cream sodas and you will."

Imogene sniffs. "I have a plan," she says.

But she doesn't say anything more about it until that night, when we're all sitting around the kitchen table at our house. For whatever reason, Miss Imogene wants to make a family announcement.

"Miss Ferguson promised me more solos this year. And she asked me—me, personally—to try out for *The King and I*."

I don't mention that Miss Ferguson offered me a solo, too, *and* said I could probably win a supporting role in the fall play. The very idea of getting on a stage makes me nauseated.

"You mean a part?" asks Dad. "A standout number, not chorus?"

Imogene leans forward conspiratorially. "I'm going to try out for Princess Tuptim."

"That's a lead, isn't it?" asks Aunt Nicole.

"Yes. The ingenue role." Aunt Nicole and Uncle Phil exchange a glance.

"What on earth does that mean?" asks Helen.

"The starry-eyed girl in love."

"How appropriate," Helen says dryly.

"What about you, Helen?" Mom asks.

"Rehearsal," she says. "And beginners' class."

"That's it?" Miss Wax pays Helen to assist with the littlest girls at the ballet studio. Imogene baby-sits for Arny in the afternoons, and Aunt Nicole has promised me more oil changes at her garage, so we'll all have money for Christmas presents and car parts, but none of us has anything to do in the evenings.

"Maybe I'll see what dance roles there are," Helen says. "As long as they don't want me to sing." Well, this is interesting. I've never known Helen to keep herself so busy.

"They won't." Imogene smiles.

"And Daisy?" asks Mom. "Now that you're in concert choir, won't they ask you to at least be in the chorus?"

"They already have," Imogene says.

I didn't know she'd heard. She's like the big ear of choir, I guess. I wonder if she's heard Tom Bixby flirting with that black-haired girl who sits next to him where the sopranos bump up against the baritones?

"I want the time for my car." I defend myself. Acting? Not for me.

"Oh, now, Daisy." Mom cajoles me. "All work and no play . . ."

"I'm saving time for the garage, too," I protest.

"Oh, don't," says Aunt Nicole. "High school comes only once."

"Thank God," says Uncle Phil.

"Daisy, you can work any Saturday you like."

I'm silent, nervous at the thought of trying out, dismal at the prospect of being excluded. If only Katrin were here . . . , I hear myself thinking for the millionth time.

"Well," I say at last, "maybe I'll do something backstage."

I'm under an engine in auto shop, working during lunch to try to figure out the secret of the perfect valve job, when I hear the voices and sounds: two boys, rustling a newspaper and scraping chairs.

"Check this out," says one. "'Sacrifice. Runs and looks good. Ask for Cindy.'"

"Oh-ho! What is it?"

"An '81 Datsun. 'Very repairable.'"

Big snort. "Go on."

"This is interesting: ''65 Dodge Dart. Needs bodywork. Only dents, no rust.'"

Mr. Fitz groans. "You don't want to know, Billy Boy!"

Oh, so it's Billy Hatcher and who, Ben? I scoot out from under (Mr. Fitz has a little creeper, a skateboard to lie on) and see Billy and Ben sitting, leaning on the back legs of their chairs, feet up on the radiator, reading a section of a newspaper that I've never seen.

"What's that?" I ask from the floor.

"Bargain News," says Ben, holding the cover up politely so I can see it.

"The 'Repairables,'" adds Mr. Fitz in solemn tones.

"Diamonds in the rough," says Ben. "Just in need of a little TLC."

"Tough luck, chump." Billy grins.

"Tender loving care." I correct him. I'm not a nurse's daughter for nothing.

"It all depends on your point of view," says Ben.

"That's a certainty," says Mr. Fitz. "From some points of view, these repairables are rat chow."

Because I have a piece of what some would call rat chow back home in my barn, I think I'll side with Ben. "What else is there?" I ask.

Ben holds up the paper to read from it.

"Oh, yes, find me a bargain," says Billy.

"'Needs to be completed, all parts there,'" reads Ben. "It's a '75 Mustang, Hatch."

"Ahh," says Billy.

With a glance at the clock, I slide back under the engine and get to work with the feeler gauge. It's pleasant work, lying there listening to them read things that might not sound as funny if I read them to myself.

"'Over $800 in mechanics' receipts. Asking $600.'"

"There's a story *there*," says Mr. Fitz.

"Oh, now lookee here. ''83 Firebird. Many extra parts. Needs mechanical work, bodywork, and interior work.'"

I snort, and loud hoots erupt from Billy. Is *he* looking for a car? Or is it Ben?

"That's not all," says Ben. "'Not running.'"

More hoots, and a howl from—from Mr. Fitz himself? Must be.

"And here's the kicker: 'Good stereo.'"

"Go forth!" bellows Mr. Fitz.

"Not done! Not done! Listen!" Ben breaks through the noise. "'Great project car.'"

"Into the universe!" Mr. Fitz finishes.

I lie on my back laughing, not getting anything done.

"How much?" asks Billy, sounding almost serious. He *is* looking for a car. But why? Just yesterday I noticed his old black Thunderbird in the student lot.

"You don't want to know," says Ben.

"Well, if it's reasonable. It's good basic material—"

"Oh, no, no, no," says Mr. Fitz.

I'm listening, listening hard. I wonder if my Beetle would have made it into the "Repairables" section. Or would it have landed in "For Sale for Parts"?

The bell rings for the end of lunch period, and I slowly pull out. Billy and Ben are on their feet, the newspaper on a chair. Ben is zipping up his backpack and heading for the door. "See you at tryouts," he says to Billy.

"What is it this year?" asks Mr. Fitz.

"The King and I," says Ben. "I'm stage manager

this year." He leaves the room.

Billy has picked up the "Repairables" again and is skimming with one finger, searching for the Firebird ad. He finds it and drops the paper in disgust. "Twenty-five hundred," he says to the floor.

I exchange a glance with Mr. Fitz.

"Don't you have a Thunderbird?" I ask, making Mr. Fitz turn his head away.

"Just a third of one," says Billy. "And that not for long."

"Where's the other part?"

"My brother Joe owns two-thirds. He has it at college. And he's making me sell off my third."

"Why?"

"Why else?" Billy shrugs. "I need the money."

I tell myself I was planning to go to tryouts anyway, that it has nothing to do with the fact that Billy and Ben are going. Ben is no surprise after all; theater is how he and Imogene started going out last year. It was during the spring show, when she was in the Cockney Chorus of *My Fair Lady* and he was on stage crew. And Billy Hatcher seems like the stage-crew type. I've just never noticed him, so he's no surprise, either, is he?

In fact, I discover he runs the lights, which I've never given a moment's thought to. I mean, apparently there's a real science to it, or so he tells me when he comes to sit in the audience beside me while we watch the tryouts for the leads and the supporting roles.

A senior, Cindy Roth, will play Anna, and the

King part goes to John Silva, a beautiful black-haired boy I've seen in concert choir. The ingenue role of Princess Tuptim is awarded to starry-eyed Imogene, and the role of Lun Tha, her lover, goes to Daniel, who sits up straight and proud at the news, with the most genuinely happy smile I've ever seen on his face. An unwelcome blush spreads across my face, and I turn away from Billy, pretending to watch intently as Helen makes her way onstage.

She gets a dance part, of course: Eliza, the lead of the ballet-within-a-play. It's really too bad Helen can't sing; she has such stage presence, just as she has in real life, a way of commanding people to look at her. When Helen is dancing, she can hardly keep from smiling every minute.

Billy watches, talking to me the whole time. "If the angles aren't just right, the whole scene can look wrong: flat, or dark, or muddy. And lights make the whole mood"—Billy can't describe this without using his hands—"scary, or sad, or morning, or sunset." It sounds like the kind of puzzle I'd like to figure out, and I hear myself saying, when Miss Ferguson calls my name for chorus, "I'm here for lighting crew, Miss F."

"Okay?" I say to Billy.

"Yeah," he says, scratching his head so that his hand nearly hides his smile, but not quite.

"I should have asked you first."

"That's all right," he says sincerely. "I'd like to get to know the nation's first red-haired, female, underage car mechanic." He has deep lines in his cheeks when he smiles.

"Oh," I say meekly, "it's not such a big deal. Practically everyone in my family knows about cars."

"Everyone?"

"Well, not my mother really. My father does his own cars, and my uncle builds race cars, and my aunt owns Auto House—"

"I get the idea. What about Helen?" He nods toward the stage. "Has she ever been known to get under a car?"

"She hasn't ever had a problem getting under a car." I defend Helen. "She changes oil, spark plugs, tires."

"Really?" Billy is incredulous. "All that, and fingernails, too?"

Poor old Helen. She does have an image to live down. Next he'll be telling me how beautiful she is.

"What about you, Daisy? Why are you so interested?"

"Because of my car," I say.

"But aren't you—" Imogene and Daniel are sitting together in the front row. I wonder if they're going to have to kiss or anything, in the play.

"Yes, just fifteen, I know. The car's a lot older than I am. I'm working on my father's old Volkswagen. As long as I can keep it running, it's mine."

"But what for?" He leans his head toward me. "Have you really driven it?"

"Well, yeah." I smile and look at the ceiling, a long way up. There's a big bar hung from it, with boxy, black stage lights bolted on.

"We're going to be working up there?" I say.

"Afraid of heights?" Billy asks.

"Not me."

The auditorium is dim except for one shaft of evening light from an open-curtained window. It lights the apron of the stage with dusty sunshine, in the midst of which is Daniel. He sits cross-legged on the marked stage floor, with his jeans jacket and a pile of books dropped carelessly beside him. The blue velvet stage curtain is closed behind him. His head is bent over his guitar. The sun lights his fair hair and his fingernails as he picks out something classical and Spanish, like ocean waves tumbling lightly over sand, like an engine running smoothly.

I sit in the front row with my geometry book in my lap and listen and watch until he knows I am there. His guitar engine slows down, turns into the driveway, and parks; a window shuts out the ocean rhythm. This is what Daniel plays when he plays for himself alone. He began playing before I came in, and he has finished with me in the room. I want to take my eyes off him but find I cannot.

Daniel rests his forearms on the side of his guitar, leans his chin on one fist, and smiles down at me. "So what'll it be, Lazy Daisy?"

I find it hard to believe, false even, that anyone would flirt with me.

"I'm not lazy," I answer stupidly. "I've been under my car all afternoon." And I've got the fingernails to prove it. Really, Daisy! How sweet! Go on and describe the whole lube job to Daniel. That'll really get him talking. I could kick myself. I could die.

What am I doing sitting here in the first place? Isn't it six o'clock yet? Where are Billy and Ben and the other stage-crew people? Miss Ferguson wanted us all here, didn't she, not just the cast? Helen dropped me off on time, I thought, even though dancers weren't yet required. Breathe deep, Daisy. I force myself to sit still, to calm down, to be here with Daniel, alone.

He looks down, pursing his lips, and finger-picks a little: Shave and a haircut, two bits! Strums a little, and sings: "Take me for a ride in your car-car, take me for a ride in your car-car, take me for a ride, take me for a ride, riding in your car-car."

I can't help smiling. Wouldn't you know that old song, Daniel? Wouldn't you pick the song my daddy used to sing when I was just a tadpole riding in the well of our purple Volkswagen?

He smiles back and sings, "Car-car goes . . ."

I look down at my bare knees poking through the holes in my jeans, and I sing with him, "beep, beep." We sing the line again, looking at each other tentatively. At the "beep, beep" I let my voice rise up to the harmony note, one octave higher, just as he drops his lower, so it blends in a pretty way, a surprise. He looks into my eyes and smiles from deep within him. He understands about the car at last, I tell myself, and wish everybody else would forget the first rehearsal.

"You should have tried out, Daisy," he says huskily, and says nothing more.

The auditorium door creaks open, letting in a world of conversation, footsteps, and Imogene.

Whang! The door slams behind her. *Whoosh!* It opens to let Ben in. I open my geometry notebook over my jeans and wave without looking up. The moment bursts, like a bubble, gone as if it never existed.

"More light," declares Billy, his voice traveling bodiless from the back of the auditorium to center stage, where I'm standing, pretending to be the King of Siam. It's period-six study hall, and we're studying lights. I shade my eyes and peer up at him.

"What for?"

His footsteps come closer, booming down the auditorium steps, taking them two at a time, until finally with one leap Billy vaults onto the stage to stand beside me.

"It's too flat," he states, waving an arm at the red-and-gold drapes and scenery meant to be the King's study. "There's not enough shadow behind the King, not enough depth in the room." He glares up at the lights.

"Daisy, take them all down to number five, will you?"

I jump off the stage and walk up to the lighting booth. Gently I move each of the ten levers on the control board from their bright levels of eight or nine down to five. On stage Billy stands watching, incongruous amid the set's grandeur in his jeans and black sneakers, pale blue shirt with its tail hanging out, and dark hair messy from running his hand through it, again and again.

"Well?" I call.

"Daisy? We need some of those big Fresnels,

with the barn-door attachments."

"We don't have any more, do we?"

"St. Mary's does. And they're not putting on a play till January. Let's go ask them."

"When? Now? I've got geometry—"

"After geometry. If we get them this afternoon, we can hang them tonight and try it out at rehearsal. Or— Oh, nuts. No car. Maybe Ben can get his mother's. Awww—" He shoves his hands in his pockets.

"We could take mine," I offer. "You'd have to drive."

Slowly Billy puts his hands on his hips, looks at me wide-eyed. "Really?"

I shrug. "It would be all right."

He grins at me. "Okay!" he says. "I'll meet you at the bus."

After geometry Billy and I ride the bus to my house. I take him into the kitchen to leave our books and to tell Mom where I'm going. She's sitting in the kitchen in the sun, with her white stocking feet up on a chair and Ezekiel in her lap.

I introduce her to Billy, and she gives him a smile.

"Want a drink?" I ask, opening the refrigerator.

"Milk, if you've got it," says Billy.

"You're the lighting genius," Mom says.

"I don't know about that," says Billy.

Mom watches him as he takes the glass from my hand. I guess he doesn't look much like any of the other boys who've been through this kitchen lately— Bixby or Daniel or Ben. His hair is still every which way, his big blue hooded sweatshirt is all warmth but

no style, and his hands are large and rough and cal-
loused and red, from what—cold? Scrubbing? Still,
my mother is glad that some boy, any boy, is here to
see me—just me. Mom watches him with a warm little
light in her eyes, and I notice that her face is pale.

"You look tired, Mom," I tell her, and she turns
her gaze to my face, silent for a moment.

"Daisy? The little Krupnik baby died today."
The Krupniks are a couple who've wanted a baby for
years and years. Their little girl was born when Mrs.
Krupnik was six months pregnant, and the baby has
been struggling for two weeks.

"Oh, Mom." I feel blank, and flat, and I have no
words at all.

Billy looks from my face to my mother's.

"I know," Mom says sadly.

The afternoon sun continues to stream in, and I
look at the kitchen clock and stand up. "I'll be back
by five," I say, hugging Mom. "I'll make some stir-fry
for dinner if you want."

"Come again, Billy," she says.

"I will," he says, surprising me, holding open the
screen door to let me through.

Billy strokes a big hand across the Beetle's hood
as gently as if it were a kitten, not a car. "This is
something, Daisy," he murmurs. "This is really
something."

"Wait'll you hear it," I tell him. I turn the key
and start her up, and Billy stands listening to the
bouncy purr of the engine.

"It sounds like it has tambourines in the hubcaps," he says.

"Jingle bells, I think. Gentle now," I tell him, moving out of the driver's seat. He slides in and does with the Beetle exactly as I tell him.

"The engine sounds a little raggedy in second," Billy tells me, shifting into third gear along Route 44.

"I told you," I say. "It's a work in progress."

"Pretty good," he says. "I'm impressed."

"It's not so much," I say.

"Don't say that. It's a lot." He pushes his hair back from his forehead, thinking.

"Your mother works at the hospital?" he asks, quiet again.

"With the premature babies," I tell him. "That one today? Her parents are as old as mine, and it was their first baby." I glance over at Billy, who's looking off across the golden fields.

"Look at that tree," he tells me, pointing out a sugar maple with a red top, orange-and-yellow middle, and leaves still green on the bottom branches.

"Like a rainbow, with the blue sky," I say.

"Do a lot of babies die?"

"Well, the ones that are most in danger get sent to Yale–New Haven," I answer. "Still, things happen unexpectedly, and sometimes there isn't time to help them."

"My mother has always wanted a girl," says Billy thoughtfully. "I guess if you had two of anything, you'd be bound to want the other kind."

"Mom says it's amazing how often people want the other kind, and they'll tell everyone that, even their children."

"Does she wish she had a boy?" asks Billy.

"She says not. She says she's seen enough to be glad she had two healthy, full-term babies, no matter what they are."

"Little baby Daisy," says Billy teasingly. "That's a good name to name a baby."

"It's just my nickname," I say staunchly. "Like Billy."

"It's William really," he answers, unabashed. "I just don't feel like a Bill or a Will or anything else. Maybe when I'm older, I'll be something different. Right now Billy is—it's just my name."

"Whatever," I say airily. It's funny to hear someone else defend his name for a change.

"Lately"—he ponders—"more people have begun calling me Bill. I didn't tell them to."

"If everyone suddenly started calling me Margaret, I don't know what I'd do," I agree.

At St. Mary's, Billy parks the Beetle outside the front entrance, and we walk inside to the music room. He introduces me to Sister Grace, a small, stout nun with curly red hair poking out from her short gray veil.

"Daisy," she says, "my hair was as long as yours when I was in high school." It looks as if it has about the same wild texture, too. I don't say that, but I don't have to. "You know," continues Sister Grace with a smile, "it's not easy to maintain my decorum with hair like this."

"It's not easy for Sister Grace to maintain her decorum anytime," Billy tells me. "You should hear her scream on dress-rehearsal night, Daisy." They talk like old friends, mocking each other.

"Never at the lighting crew," denies Sister Grace. "Speaking of which, dearie, I gather your fall play is upon you?"

"A play has fallen upon him," I say, and they both laugh.

"I only visit Sister Grace when I want something," admits Billy.

"Oh, now and then he makes a social call," Sister Grace tells me. She makes a deal with Billy to lend him six Fresnels and a big box of gels, and we load them into the backseat of the Beetle, atop the Cornell blanket.

"Don't break your neck, Billy," calls Sister Grace, waving at us from the sidewalk. "I'll need you in January."

"Do you do lights at St. Mary's, too?" I ask as we drive away.

"Now and then." He shrugs one shoulder. "I like Sister Grace."

"So do I."

Back at school we fill the lighting booth with the heavy black lights with their cranky barn-door flaps, dust our hands on our jeans, and trudge back to the Beetle.

"Are you going to paint it?" asks Billy.

"No, just wax," I say. "I like the purple, like a big bug." I put out my hand. "Keys," I say.

"That's appropriate," allows Billy, ignoring my hand. "Someone's already waxed a bit." He indicates the fender.

"Daniel," I answer, and stupidly I blush.

Billy looks straight at me with clear gray eyes

and seems to nod without moving his head. "Schweitzer?"

I look away. It's awkward for a moment; then Billy tosses me my keys.

"Okay," I say. "I'm up to it."

"You driving?"

"Sure," I say, for no good reason.

"But—" He snatches them back. I lunge at his hand, but miss.

"I know what I'm doing," I tell him, lying. He slowly places the key ring in my palm.

I nod. "Just to my house. You're of age. You can say you're teaching me. It's only two miles."

Billy gets into the passenger seat wordlessly. I get in behind the wheel and start up my car. I ease her down the school driveway and pull out onto Route 44. The road east is thick with rush-hour traffic. Careful to obey the speed limit, I drive the two miles along Route 44, a line of impatient commuters forming behind me. I'm signaling for the turn for our driveway when I hear the noise: a little bump, a bang, then nothing further unusual. Billy listens closely also, with a strange expression on his face.

I turn the car into our driveway, and Billy says, "What was that?"

"I'm not sure," I say slowly, unwilling to admit that I haven't the least idea. I park outside the barn where I can easily turn the floodlight on to have a look after Billy has gone. Helen is sitting in her Renault, looking as if she has just gotten home.

A yellow Jeep pulls into the driveway behind us, with a dark-haired woman at the wheel.

"That's my mother," Billy says, not moving.

"Great! Well, I'll see you tonight," I say. I jump out and walk toward the Jeep.

"Daisy, wait." Billy still stands beside my car. "Shouldn't we take a look under the hood?"

"I'll take care of it," I tell him, trying to sound casual. "Your mother probably wants to go." She does. She's got her window down, and she's waving Billy toward her. I recognize her as one of the people who works at Hendries', the garden place where my mother buys her lilies. I dart into the kitchen, grab Billy's books, and practically throw them at him. "See you tonight," I say again.

"Okay. Let me know if you need any help. All right, Daisy?"

"Sure." But I'm not sure at all. If something is wrong with my car, I want to be the one to discover what it is, to take that first frightening peek under the hood. If something's wrong, I'll fix it. I'm not anyone's little girl mechanic anymore. All summer long I've got this car working so that now it's good and smooth and harmonious and flowing. If there's a glitch, I'll find it.

Yet my mind is full of frightening shouldn't-haves: shouldn't have taken the car so far, shouldn't have driven it home, shouldn't have been trying to impress Billy. I try to tell myself that whatever happened would have happened no matter who was driving the car.

With a glance toward the kitchen—I've got to hurry and start dinner—I snap on the floodlight against the deepening dusk and lift the hood.

Oh, God. Something wrong? Something's disastrous. There's oil everywhere. I dive underneath and spy a few drips of oil dropping into the driveway, where more drops show as black spots in the dirt. I check the oil level—barely any. Where is it all? Down the road a piece? What did I do, hit a rock? On my back under the car I shine my flashlight up. No holes. Not even a dent or a crack or a scratch. I pull myself out and stare into the engine, make a few halfhearted swipes with a rag over the oiliest places.

Over my shoulder, Helen says, "What's up?"

I sigh and close the hood abruptly. "Not sure," I answer. "Help me push it into the barn, will you?" She sets down her ballet bag on the back steps. I sit in the driver's seat for a moment, release the hand brake, shift to neutral, and fight back tears.

Helen and I lean against the front bumper and push the Beetle slowly into the barn. "Correct me if I'm wrong," she says carefully, "but weren't you driving just now?"

"I didn't do anything to it, Helen," I growl. Dad's headlights catch us in their beams as we get the car into place.

"Don't say anything," I say quickly.

"Why not?" Helen retorts.

"Just don't," I tell her fiercely, and lean against the car's big bulgy front.

"What's new, pumpkins?" asks Dad. He balances his leather briefcase on his head, steadying it with one hand. The floodlight over his head leaves his face in shadow.

"Nothing," I say, attempting to sound cheerful.

Helen lounges against the bumper beside me. "Same old junk," she says.

Dad looks at us for a moment. "Anything wrong?"

"No," we say in unison.

"Tell Mom we'll be there in a minute," I call.

"Okay." He gives us another puzzled look and goes up the steps.

"Helen?" I say quietly. "The Krupniks' baby died today."

"Oh, no." She covers her mouth with the heel of her hand. "Was it—"

"I don't know what," I say, "or why."

Helen stares across the darkening meadow, then turns and looks into my eyes. She pats the bumper and can't stop herself from being curious. "And what's with this Bug?" she asks grimly.

"Don't say anything about the car," I warn her. "Whatever it is, I'll take care of it."

"Whatever it is?" she repeats. Across the meadow among the dark trees, an owl calls.

"Shut up, Helen," I whisper.

She stares at me then. "I'm in the act of shutting up," she says abruptly. "I'm shutting up as I speak." She turns and walks briskly into the house.

I stand alone in the dark, waiting to hear the owl call again. I would like to walk up the meadow to the woods and stand under the trees, listening for the owl. What I did is what I did—not Billy's fault. And I can't help remembering the way Billy stroked the gleaming wing of my Beetle, as tenderly as if it were the wing of a dragonfly that lit on his arm.

* * *

"Where were you?" Billy demands. "We were going to have those lights hung an hour ago."

"Sorry." He bugs his eyes out at me. "Can't we hang them now?"

"Yeah," he says, shutting his eyes and scratching his head. "But we won't get to see how it looks until next week."

"I'm sorry," I say again, uselessly. His hands stuffed in his pockets, he studies my face.

"So what's with the car?"

"I don't know," I say. "Oil everywhere."

Billy frowns. "Cracked sump? But you didn't hit anything."

"No. No cracks or holes or anything, but there's no oil, either."

"I'll take a look at it if you want me to," Billy volunteers.

"That's all right," I tell him, fingering the lighting notebook in my lap, not looking at him.

There's a cool pause. Then he says, "Fine," and, "I'm going to hang some lights now, Daisy."

He hooks a Fresnel over his arm and climbs up the ladder, terrifyingly high above the stage. How Billy does like to be in control of matters! Well, for that matter, so do I.

Below Billy, Imogene is onstage, in the King's study, being introduced to the King. Imogene has always been apt to fall over her own feet, but not here, not now. She's too tall, too blonde to be a Burmese princess, but she makes her movements small and delicate, and speaks her lines with a slightly British, slightly Asian accent that's just a little phony.

Watching Imogene onstage, I stand feeling graceless and large. Beside Billy (beside his ladder, actually) I stand feeling ignorant and undedicated, too casual and untalented for a play like this. Yet, if I were home in the barn with my head under my car's hood, I would feel a thousand times worse. So I stay.

Where did my oil go?

I can't run the engine without it.

I have to find the problem. I will find the problem. But how?

After the weekend, in the Monday-afternoon daylight, when no one is home, I lift the hood and survey the damage. For there must be damage somewhere. Oil seems to have sprayed out sideways and upward, all over the right side of the engine. Everything is gooey, from the top of the carburetor on down. I take a rag from the box and begin to wipe the engine clean. It's going to take me just forever, but maybe by going slowly and carefully, going over every millimeter of this engine that I already know by heart, I'll find the trouble. All week I argue with myself. For the first time in a long time, it's hard to resist asking Dad to have a look. But if he does, he'll find the problem, and I'll learn nothing. And he might find out that I was driving. Then it'll be back to the icehouse for my Beetle. In spite of his own driving record, and maybe *because* of it, Dad would take a dim view of what I've done, I'm certain. I can't lie and tell him Billy was driving; then he might want to talk to Billy. I can't think of anything to do that isn't somehow all wrong, and as the week goes by, it just gets worse.

At rehearsal Billy has trouble directing the lights for the effect that he wants. It doesn't help that I show up late again, taking the time to work on my car while Dad's working late one night. I hang the portable light above the engine and poke my way slowly around the valves, wiping and feeling delicately with my fingertips. Mom's face startles me, appearing suddenly under the lamp.

"Well, Daisy," she trills, "what are we doing?"

"A little investigation, Ma."

"Of . . . ?"

"Don't worry, Mom. I'm just messing around."

"Well," she says, with a skeptical look, "I thought I should tell you it's seven-thirty. You were going to call me when you wanted a ride to rehearsal?"

"Oh, no!" I shut the hood fast, wipe my hands on my jeans, and dive into the Mustang.

Mom drops me off in front of the high school. Inside, Billy is already dangling from a pipe atop the A-frame ladder. He glowers down at me. When he descends to pick a gel from the box, he turns a flushed face toward me.

"Let me guess." He confronts me. "Car trouble?"

"Still," I say wearily.

"I'm having crew trouble myself," he says. "It's like this. I climb the ladder. I hang a light, then I climb down again to turn on the light. I climb back up to adjust the light. I come down and get Ben or someone who ought to be doing something else to stand where I want the light to hit. Then I climb back up to direct the light, and Miss Ferguson calls Ben to come pull the curtain. So I climb down—"

"I get the picture," I stop him. "I'm sorry. I'm trying to squeeze everything in."

"Don't get huffy, Daisy," Billy says gently. "Just get here." I don't like him bossing me, even if he is technically the boss.

Silently I watch the action onstage, where all the King's children and Anna sing "Getting to Know You." Helen mouths the words, no sound coming out. The children and Anna exit from the classroom set, leaving Imogene, as Tuptim, onstage. Daniel, as her boyfriend, creeps in and spies her there, and they run to each other's arms. Spare me. What am *I* doing *here*?

"Why don't you let me help?" Billy touches the back of my hand with his index finger.

"No," I gulp. "I can't." Not him. Not anyone.

"Freckles," Billy remarks, examining my hand.

"Come on," I tell him, forcing a smile to my lips. "Hang lights, Hatcher." He rolls his eyes and picks out a blue gel, trots back up his ladder. Through the hallway door I catch sight of Helen, practicing a ribbon dance. Onstage Imogene and Daniel sing a duet, a love song. I stand below the ladder and watch Billy for a signal.

It is late that Friday night, when the wind tosses leaves from the trees and little clouds fly in the face of the moon, that Helen quietly opens the kitchen door, throws her bag and coat on the floor, sits down on the back stairs, and cries. From my window I watch the taillights of Tom Bixby's mother's station wagon disappear down the driveway and turn west on Route 44, toward town.

I pad down the stairs in my socks and sit beside Helen, speechless and chilled. She pulls a tissue from her pocket and blows her nose noisily. Looking at her hands, she manages to say, "Tom broke up with me."

"Why?" I ask incredulously.

"Helen?" Mom appears at the top of the stairs in her flannel pajamas and, seeing Helen's upturned white face, comes down to sit behind her. Ezekiel follows Mom and rubs against Helen's leg. "What's wrong?"

"Oh, Ma!" Helen moans, lays her head on Mom's knees, and begins to cry again.

Mom smiles a sad little smile at me and shakes her head. She strokes Helen's head, and I stroke Ezekiel's.

"It's Bixby," I say by way of explanation.

"Tell me," Mom says to Helen.

After a minute Helen lifts her head. "He says he never loved me," she gulps. "He said it was so wonderful to be with me that he thought he was in love. Then I guess he met two girls this summer and realized that he wanted to be with other people, too."

"Why couldn't he?" Maybe I shouldn't ask. Not one girl, two!

"Because of me," sobs Helen. "He says I love him so much, I'm too serious all the time. But how can I be lighthearted about it? I want to be with him at a party. I don't want to stand there eating a hot dog and watching him throw Darlene Macomber in the leaves. I mean, what am I supposed to do, laugh? He says I've gotten too serious to throw in the leaves. He says I'm so pretty he doesn't want to mess me up. He thinks I want to be married or something, and he just wants to hang around with everyone. How can he feel that way, Mom?"

"I don't know, babe," Mom answers. She probably really doesn't know. She met Dad when she was almost as young as Helen, and I bet he never said he wanted to go off with other girls. "If he's saying that sort of thing, I think maybe you'd better look elsewhere, Hel."

"I don't have any choice!" Helen says coldly. She grasps her elbows, shivering, and I remember her on the Fourth of July, her T-shirt rolled up to bare her shoulders to the sun, playing baseball, taking a lead off second, while Bixby, pitching, tried to hold her on base. In the end he got exasperated, ran over, picked her up, and carried her back to the bag. She shrieked at him then, with happiness and exasperation, and wound up falling in the dirt, sweaty and covered in dust, while Bixby laughed down at her. Nobody called her too serious or too pretty then.

Mom walks Helen up to bed, and I snuggle under my comforter again, eyes wide open. After a while through the wall I hear Mom go to bed, hear her voice quietly explaining things to Dad, and I hear Dad's gruff, indignant response.

Oh, Helen! I picture tall, dark, blue-eyed Bixby in his red-sleeved baseball shirt and his glasses, his ancient, ageless glove, always so handsome, always so kind to me and, I thought, to Helen. He didn't mean to be unkind to Helen now, I think. He was just being honest, not wanting to hurt her anymore, wanting to be free of her. How much more awful to lose someone as handsome as Bixby, who was once hers, than it would be for me to lose someone, anyone, even Daniel. What could I know about it? Daniel isn't mine at all, so I haven't got anything, anyone to lose.

october

STORYBOOK HALLOWEEN HOP reads the orange-and-white poster outside the auto shop. HOP ON IN DRESSED AS YOUR FAVORITE STORYBOOK CHARACTER.

Well. It's the first big party of the year, and even though I'm not exactly Miss School Spirit, I don't intend to miss this. What will I go as? I can't imagine. Cinderella? My feet are too big. The Cheshire Cat? Possibly; I'm not sure how to look partially disappeared, although it's an appealing thought. Medusa, with snakes in my hair? No one will know who I am unless they took mythology for ninth-grade English. Mother Goose herself? An animal, that's the ticket.

Someone's hands are in my hair, holding my head so I can't turn it. "Rapunzel," Billy says. He lifts my hair and softly kisses the back of my neck. I jump and elbow him, and he lets me go.

"Knock it off!" I say furiously, hot and cold with embarrassment. At that moment Mr. Fitz opens the shop door, and I find a chair well away from Billy's.

It's a sit-down class, thank goodness, and I bury my head in my notebook, meeting only Mr. Fitz's eyes as I answer questions about engine temperature and combustion. In the middle of the class a small piece of yellow paper drops into my lap. I unfold it under the desk and read: "I didn't think you'd mind so much."

I turn to frown at Billy, who shrugs one shoulder a little sheepishly. My mind wanders away from engine explosions to daydream that I am driving my Beetle down a sunlit road, all alone, free and independent and at least two years older, very far away from everything and everyone and especially Billy Hatcher.

Imogene's car is in the shop, and she needs a ride to play rehearsal. Helen and I drive the Renault into town to pick her up, and I graciously climb into the backseat to give her the front. As I'm climbing in, she asks, all flustered, "Would it be okay to pick up Daniel? He asked me for a ride, and I couldn't say no, even if my car is out of commission. Do you mind?" Helen shrugs and turns the car around to drive back out of town on Route 44, to Daniel's condominium. Imogene jumps out of the car and runs to knock on the door.

"Should I move, do you think?" I ask Helen.

"Nah," says Helen nastily. So Daniel squeezes in the back with me.

Thank goodness that the dark hides the expression on my face. We are both way too tall for the backseat. Every nerve ending in my body stands at attention, feeling Daniel's shoulder wedged against mine, his kneecap mashed against my calf.

"Well," says Daniel, "about this party. I can't think of any storybook characters that would suit my personality. Does it have to be a real story? Couldn't it be something from movies or TV?"

"The Jolly Green Giant?" Helen suggests helpfully.

Imogene says, "Well, he's not *that* tall."

"A wandering minstrel?" I put in.

"Something evil," Daniel wishes. "A villain, in a cape and mustache."

"You're too benevolent," I say softly.

But Helen hears. "And too blond."

Daniel glances at his reflection in the rearview mirror, arches his eyebrows, and furrows them into a deep glare. He growls. "The Big Bad Wolf!" he snarls.

"Ideal," Imogene agrees. "Put gray streaks in your hair and tease it up all wild."

"A gray sweater and jeans and a big bushy tail," Helen adds.

"Claws," I say. The idea is growing on me.

"And big teeth!"

"Who are you going to get to be the three little pigs?" I ask.

"Wrong story," growls Daniel, making his hands into claws at me. "Red Riding Hood!"

"I could wear a long red cape," says Imogene.

"And do your hair in pipe curls," Daniel says, getting even more enthusiastic.

"You're more like Goldilocks," says Helen. Yeah, I think, Goldilocks sneaking into someone's house to take his porridge.

We pull up (at last) behind the school. "No," says Imogene as Helen turns off the engine. "Red Riding Hood often has blonde curls." We unfold ourselves from the car (Daniel gives me his hand) and walk across the parking lot. In my book at home Red Riding Hood has long brown braids.

I leave the others in the front row of the auditorium and slink into the lighting booth. I drop my coat on a chair beside Billy's. With his back to me, he sits studying the lighting board, shifting a switch here, a lever there. I look out at the auditorium, where Daniel and Imogene sit with their fair heads together, dreaming up their Halloween costumes.

"About this morning?" Billy says without turning. "Something just came over me."

I can't think of a single thing to say. Watching Daniel out there giggling with Imogene, I ought to be glad someone, anyone, wants to kiss my neck. But why does it have to be Billy? I like him. We're friends. But when I'm not with Billy, I don't think about him all that much. It's not his hair that I picture, not the back of his neck. It's not his hands that I imagine.

"It passed anyway," Billy says, turning to look at me. "I no longer have the urge."

"Good," I say weakly. He shows me what he's been doing with the lights then, and I ask him, "What are you going to the Halloween party as?" I've got to say something. It's going to be a tough six weeks backstage if I don't.

Billy is silent for a moment, tinkering with a switch. "I was thinking of something invisible," he says, "like the Invisible Man."

"Or Harvey, the giant rabbit?" He gives me a questioning look, and his expression grows a little brighter as I tell him the story of that old James Stewart movie. "But how—"

"Easy," says Billy. He has been waiting for me to ask. "You know, I'm a master of special effects. Being invisible is going to be a piece of cake."

Saturday morning I wake up late, after a long strange sleep of bad dreams. The house is empty. I drink a giant glass of orange juice in the kitchen, determined to wash out my head. I pull my lucky shoes over my bare feet and take the porch steps, running. Wouldn't you know it? The whole family is in the barn. Don't they ever do anything but work on cars? Isn't there a football game they could go to? A harvest fair? A car show?

I do my best to ignore them. I stride straight into the barn and pop up the Beetle's hood. "Hi, Daze." Helen is there with a rag, checking the oil in the Renault. Dad and Uncle Phil have the Saab hood up, and their heads underneath it. Aunt Nicole is helping Mom winterize her Mustang, pulling up the convertible top. Black plastic antifreeze jugs litter the dirt floor.

I can even hear Imogene out in the meadow behind the barn, patiently arguing with Arny: "For the last time, do you want to hide or seek? Tell me!"

Helen announces, "I'm going to be Glinda, the Good Witch, for Halloween."

"Honestly." I laugh. "Why not the Wicked Witch of the West?"

"I might melt. I've always wanted Glinda's big hat anyway. What about you? Any ideas yet?"

"I don't know."

I try to picture myself in a costume. Rapunzel? My hair isn't fabulous enough, just long and bright. I am tall and broad shouldered and angular, and my face is nothing special.

The time that I think I felt most beautiful was one of those early days of summer, the first or second day of July. I woke up early, before anyone else, and walked outside in my bare feet and one of Dad's big old flannel shirts. The grass was dewy and the air was soft, and my hair hung in clouds around my shoulders. I walked down the meadow to the side of the icehouse and picked raspberries. They were cool and sweet, and the bushes were full of daddy longlegs and flexible green prickers and night air, and I imagined that someone like Daniel could see me, and that he fell in love just watching me.

Now, in cold October, I see in my Beetle's sideview mirror nothing that goes along with the raspberry morning in my head. It is in this moment that I decide to go to the Storybook Halloween Hop as a frog.

"I'm going to be a frog," I announce to the barn. If I talk, maybe they won't notice that I'm standing here staring into the engine of my car, feeling as mixed up as ever.

"Which frog?" asks Helen. "The little frog that grants wishes to queens?"

"Sleeping Beauty," I respond. "No."

"The frog prince?" Uncle Phil asks. "Or frog

princess?" Saved by a kiss? Not me.

"The frog footman, from *Alice in Wonderland*," suggests my mother.

"Neither nor," I answer.

In spite of the trouble, I have my engine looking pristine again, and I don't see any big difference, although I peer at it from every angle. I have to concentrate hard to stay focused, though; there's a hollow spot of fear in my stomach that seems to burn larger every day that this problem doesn't get solved.

Out of the corner of my eye I see my father walk over and talk to Helen, their heads together behind the Renault's dark green hood. I flop down on my back and use my feet to push myself under the Beetle.

I poke and prod and peer at the underside, then drop my head back on the ground with a sigh. How can there be an invisible problem? I lie there, not knowing what to think. I see bears in my mind, crawling into their winter caves and burrows. Does it feel a lot different from the dirt of this barn floor? Could I solve this problem if I could just get a little extra sleep?

"I don't know." I hear Helen's muffled voice. "She wouldn't tell me, either."

Dad says something unintelligible.

"Just a lot of oil everywhere," says Helen, loud and clear.

I pull myself out from under the car and flip back my braid. Helen and Aunt Nicole are watching me. I look back at them for a moment, then look away.

Dad appears at my elbow. "So what's eating the Bug?" he asks cheerfully.

"It's nothing much," I say, too hastily.

"Oh?" Dad purses his lips. "Seems like I haven't heard that happy little engine run for a while."

"No," I say, praying he won't ask to hear it now. "Just a little glitch, Daddy. And I'm going to solve it myself."

He looks stung, and I'm instantly sorry.

"That's what you get!" Uncle Phil's voice booms across the barn. "You've created a prodigy, John. Now you have to live with it!"

"Her," my mother says.

"That's the *deal*," I announce to them all. "My car. My work." It's kind of a new deal, actually, with new rules. I watch closely to see how Dad will take it.

A scattering of feelings crosses my father's face. He doesn't know whether to be proud of me, or to yell at me, to laugh, or just to walk away. As for me, I want to do all those things, plus a few more involving tears. I feel I've crossed some invisible line. There's no going back to being the child apprentice. Yet the car is—what? Dead?

The barn phone rings, and we all stand there and look at it. Imogene bursts through the door and snatches the phone off the wall. "Daisy?" she says. "It's Billy Hatcher." And she bats her eyelashes at me. I look in confusion from Imogene's face to Dad's and see in the glance the eyes of my mother and uncle and aunt, watching me.

"Oh, Daisy," says Helen in exasperation, "why don't you just—"

"Why don't you just butt out?" I say to her, to all

of them. I slam down the Beetle's hood rudely and run into the kitchen to get the phone there.

"Hello? Billy?"

"Daisy? So what are you going to be?"

What am I going to be? For a minute there he's got me stumped.

"An amphibian," I say at last. "A green animal that lives partly on land, partly in the water."

"Uh," says Billy. "A turtle?"

"Wrong."

"Well. What I want to know is, can I give you a ride to the Halloween party?"

"A ride?" In what car? My stupid mind is whirling. In the driveway Dad is talking—no, con- ferring—with Aunt Nicole, Helen and Imogene at her side. Arny comes up the steps with his knees brown and green from the meadow, opens the refrig- erator, and hands me the orange juice.

"A date, if you want to call it that, but I thought you might not want to call it that. Call it a ride if it makes you feel better, Daisy." I open the cupboard and bring out a blue plastic cup.

How does he know what I feel? I pour the juice and hand it to Arny, who gives me a thumbs-up sign.

"All right." Anything not to rely on Helen or Imogene for transportation. And I don't mind the idea of a frog and the Invisible Man going to the party together. "As long as you promise to stay invisible."

"Maybe I will. Maybe I won't." Cute. That's what Helen would say.

"Okay," I tell him. Let's ride, Billy. Away. Anywhere far.

"Good. I'll talk to you next week."

"Bye."

Mom comes out of the barn, walks into the kitchen, and scrubs her hands at the sink. "Arny?" she asks pleasantly. "Help Daisy make us a salad for lunch, would you, babe? You can tear up the lettuce."

There have been times when I've shared the bathroom mirror with Helen and wondered, What is it like to be inside her skin, to look out of her eyes and hair and see her face, instead of mine? Now I wouldn't want to be inside her skin for anything. Her sadness is so sad it makes me shudder, it makes it hard to be in the same room with her, it makes me hold her off at arm's length, not talking about anything really, just costumes and teachers and the play, for fear that if I get her onto the wrong subject, she'll dissolve into tears again.

For the party Helen curls her straight brown hair into a froth of frizz, and the coffee can on her head is completely disguised with silver fabric and glitter. She is surrounded by yards and yards of dusky pink tulle, adapted from some old ballet costume. With her wand she taps Arny on his head. "They're called Munchkins!" she says in a sugary sweet imitation of the "real" Glinda.

"Cut it out!" says Arny. He swings around crossly, swatting Mom with his Batman cape. Too young for anything more than trick or treat, Arny is going to spend the evening with Mom and Dad, while Uncle Phil and Aunt Nicole take the train to New

York for the Halloween parade.

Imogene is, after all, a splendid Red Riding Hood. Her hood and cape are bright red felt, covering a checkered green dress, knee socks, and Mary Janes. Her hair is done in precise sausage curls, her cheeks painted falsely pink with freckles.

My costume, from the bottom up, consists of Mom's yellow scuba flippers (talk about disguising my big feet), green tights and leotard borrowed from Helen, with yellow felt dots sewn to the back, and makeup, complete with huge black eyes and green skin, designed by Helen and executed by me. My hair is braided into huge bumps atop my head and coated with Vaseline and green powdered poster paint. Imogene has brought me a gift from Uncle Phil, a pair of his shiny yellow racing gloves, each finger outfitted with a bright white suction cup.

"Inventive!" Helen admires them.

"That was really nice of him," I say, impressed.

"So, Daisy," Imogene asks coyly, "this 'ride' with Billy, is this a date?"

"No," I tell her coolly. "We're just friends." But, I ask myself, are we?

We stand in the hallway and look in the mirror: Red Riding Hood, a good witch, a frog, and Batman. Mom comes in with a bowl of Baby Ruths and Jujyfruits, and Helen automatically reaches for them.

"Watch it!" Mom swats Helen's hand away.

"Are you sure Billy thinks of it that way?" from Imogene, reaching a stealthy hand toward the candy.

"Oh, go ahead, each of you have one," Mom relents.

"I'm not sure what he thinks," I say. "I just know what I think."

"And what's that?" asks Mom gently.

"That it's enough to be *with* someone because he's nice or friendly or interesting."

Imogene looks at Helen and snickers, but Helen shakes her head in reply.

"That's not enough for me!" Imogene sings out. I don't want to hear about it.

"Well, fine," Helen retorts. "You just be you. Let everyone else be—"

"Just because you're *with* someone doesn't mean you're in love with him. Or in lust," I say hotly, my eyes on Imogene, who's busy unwrapping a Baby Ruth and doesn't look up.

Outside Billy's mother's yellow Jeep pulls up, and something odd looking looms from the driver's seat and lurches up the kitchen steps. It looks like a man, extremely tall, with no face, just his hat floating on the air where the top of his head should be. He's wearing gloves but has no wrists; the gloves are floating, like the hat. Arny lets out a screech and throws himself upon Imogene.

The top buttons of the man's coat part, and Billy puts his head out. "Hey," he says to Arny, "I'm real. It's okay."

"You're real, all right." My mother laughs.

"I think we'd better go," I say, with a look at Arny's face, half hidden inside Imogene's red cape.

"See you," I tell them. I slap across the porch in my flippers.

Billy walks ahead of me to the Jeep. At the top of

the steps Helen catches my arm.

"I know why you didn't want to go with me and Imogene," she whispers. "I should warn you, Imogene's planning on having a good time with Daniel tonight."

I nod. "I figured as much. Helen?" I ask. "I really don't know what's going to happen with Billy. I like him, but—"

"It's all right then," she says. "Go have fun. And if you need a ride home, just whistle."

Billy and I must make quite a picture, an invisible man at least seven feet tall, and a frog with gigantic flippers that take up half the dance floor. The gym is decorated in orange and white streamers and tiny yellow Christmas lights. Giant Connecticut pumpkins line the doorways. The overhead lamps are set at low, and the glow from the Christmas lights is enough to make out the happy, smug expression on Imogene's face as she dances with Daniel. He's huge in his wolf costume, with big, fluffy ears and a long tail, his eyes hidden behind a furry mask.

Someone starts a conga line, and Billy and I join in. I grab on to his coat and realize it's the first time I've touched him. It's not exactly romantic, but he's nice, Billy is, and with him I never have to think about whether what I'm going to say sounds smart or stupid, because he likes me, smart or stupid or somewhere in between. I like his sense of humor, too, his overcoat buttoned over his invisible head, and the big derby wired on top, and white gloves like Mickey Mouse's. I look to see whether he's holding on to the girl in front of him with his real hands or his gloves. True to form, he's pretending to hold on with his gloves. I laugh and give up being self-conscious and turn my mind to having a good time.

I pass Helen in the conga line, weaving through the crowd in her fluffy Good Witch dress, her hat made from an enormous silver coffee can. She's dancing between two senior boys I don't know but recognize, baseball players dressed as bumblebees. Beyond the line couples are dancing: Bixby, dressed as a pirate, and that dark-haired girl from concert choir, wearing a teddy-bear costume. Imogene dances with Daniel, who's wolfishly nibbling her neck—not a necessary part of the act, if you ask me.

It gets a little difficult dancing in scuba flippers, and when I drop into a chair at the end of the conga dance, Billy looks ready to join me.

"I'm dying of heat," he says. "Let's go outside for a minute, okay?" On the way out of the gym we pass a giant blue Cookie Monster who turns out to be Ben.

"Hey, Bill," he says. "Daisy, dance with me when you come back, will you? I've been looking for Kermit all night."

"Okay." I laugh.

"That's fine with me, Daisy," says Billy. "This isn't a date, it's a ride, remember?"

I smile at him, a little uncertain. What was that I was saying about being so comfortable with Billy? I take it back.

The air outside is cool and crisp, and the fall wind brings crunchy leaves up around our feet (flippers) as we sit down on the stone wall.

"Why did you come as a frog, Daisy?" asks Billy.

"Well, they said it was a Hop."

"No, really." He unbuttons the top of his coat and sticks his head out comically.

"Why did you come as the Invisible Man?" I counter.

"It suits my personality," says Billy. "I'm the behind-the-scenes man, right?"

"But things wouldn't happen if you weren't there," I protest. "And those things are visible. Without your lights, all the people on the stage would be invisible."

"Maybe they should be," says Billy darkly. "Nobody sees me, one way or the other."

And maybe he likes it that way, I think angrily. Maybe it's what he wants—to be the man who pushes the buttons, unseen, who makes the lights go on, like the Great and Powerful Oz. Yet I remember what he said after he told Mr. Fitz that I'd rebuilt my car's engine: "That's more than most of us have done."

"It makes me mad that you think you're not important." I persist. "The lights you turn on, the engines you work on, those are important things. They don't happen by magic, you know."

"Maybe they do," says Billy. "Say what you might, you think it's all magic sometimes, don't you, Daisy?" His voice has an unfamiliar hard edge to it.

"What do you mean?" My legs begin to shiver in the new autumn cold.

"Take this car of yours. You worked on it all summer long, right?" I nod my big green head. "Even got to drive it a few times, right? But now it's not working. You think that all you have to do is clean things up and scrub off the rust, then close your eyes and wish and the problem will go away."

"I do not," I cry indignantly. "You know yourself that once I find the problem and fix it, it'll run again!"

"How do you know what I know?" He crosses his arms, his real arms, his fake gloves flopping out at his sides, and stares up the hill to the swings, where a black cat and a bumblebee are swinging. The sound of their laughter floats down to our ears.

I stand up to face him, beginning to shiver from my stomach upward.

"And what do you know, Billy Hatcher?" He's just like Uncle Phil and Aunt Nicole and Dad, thinking he knows everything and wanting to tell me what to do.

"It's a goner, Daisy." He shakes his head seriously, his voice authoritative now. "You spend half your life with your head inside that engine, and where is it getting you? You ought to junk it, Daisy. Find another engine to put your heart and soul into. That car's been sitting in that icehouse too long!"

"How can you say that?" I'm shouting now, and as I hear this noise coming out of my mouth, something goes quiet inside my head. He's trying to hurt me because I've hurt him, pushing away his kiss, making his date just a ride, rebuilding a car engine before him—and then refusing to let him help me when it blew.

"It's as good as dead, Daisy," Billy says. "You

think you know so much about it all, and up to a point I'm willing to go along with you. But not anymore."

"Fine," I yell. "You don't have to go along with me anywhere. I never asked you to. I'll get my own ride home." I leave him then, stomp inside to the girls' room.

When I go back into the gym, Billy is nowhere to be seen, truly invisible now, ha. The party is breaking up. The band members are packing away their instruments in sparkling blue cases, and Daniel and his guitar have been fooling around at the microphone. He taps it to make sure it's working and croons a song about the end of a party.

Why did I dress as a frog? Maybe deep down I hoped I'd be the kind of frog that magically turned into something or someone else. Daniel certainly isn't going to make it happen with a kiss. The way he's been dancing and snuggling with Imogene is proof enough to me that I'm not one bit in the picture, me and my sunset hair, presently dyed green. And it sure isn't going to be Billy. He's kissed me once, and I still don't know why. He'll probably never try it again. And somehow that thought makes me feel lonely to the soles of my flippers.

Helen drives me home, blessedly asking no questions. Imogene arrives close behind us; she's spending the night since her parents won't be back till late. I watch her come through the kitchen door, flushed and happy.

"You missed Daniel singing 'I'm in Love with a Big Blue Frog,' Daisy," she announces.

Helen sighs. "That Daniel. And poor Daisy. He shouldn't tease you."

My neck grows hot. "Tease me? Imogene, has Daniel been making fun of me?"

"Oh, not so anyone else would know. Helen's right. He shouldn't have. But it *is* a funny song."

"Daniel chooses his songs better than that," I say. "He wouldn't sing 'I Dream of Jeanie' to you if he didn't do some dreaming, Imogene."

Helen moves to stand behind me, with her hands on the back of my chair. "So you think he's trying to tell you something?" she asks me.

"Like what?" I ask. Helen begins to take hairpins out of my braids and let them down.

Gingerly Imogene says, "Well, you *have* been getting a little bit boring about that Volkswagen, Daisy." I stiffen, but Helen's hands smooth my hair, unbraiding. "And Daniel must resent your coming to see his father so much."

"That's silly! His father is there for the asking."

"Only if you're asking about oval-window Volkswagen Bugs, Daisy. Daniel's bound to be jealous."

Helen's voice is calm. "What makes you think you're right, Imo?"

"He told me," she admits. "I was at his house practicing our scenes." I'll bet. Imagine Imogene, at Daniel's house among the car magazines and sheet music, the beige sofa, the fireplace with its warm gray stones.

"What did he say?" I ask grimly.

"That his father wishes he had a son like you."

A compliment from Daniel's father would have warmed me from the toes up a few months ago, but now my ears are listening for Daniel's words.

"A son like Daisy? Why not a daughter? Because girls aren't supposed to know mechanics?" Helen sputters. "Does it follow that boys shouldn't know music?"

"I guess that's what Daniel's father thinks," Imogene confirms.

"And Daniel? And you?" I ask accusingly.

"It's all right, Daisy," Helen implores me.

"No, it's not all right, Helen!" I spark. "It's all right for Imogene to know nothing about cars and be Miss Feminine, as long as she has all of us around to change her oil! And it's all right for Imogene to sit there and listen to Daniel make fun of me, but why? All in the interest of eliminating the competition, right? Because you like him just as much as I do, right?"

Imogene, with her hands on her gingham hips, shakes her head, trying to laugh it off. "Well, of course you're right, Daisy Do," she says. "Aren't you always?" Her cheeks turn naturally red now under her pink makeup. Flustered, she turns and walks down the hall into the bathroom, slamming the door behind her.

Helen doesn't know what to do with herself. She picks up our tea mugs off the table and all but throws them into the sink. "You know something, Daisy?" she asks angrily. "You don't do yourself any favors. What do you want someone like Daniel for anyway?"

"Why shouldn't I?" I cry. "Because he's beautiful and I'm not?"

Helen sits down across from me and leans over to grab my wrist. "Beautiful?" she repeats. "What's beautiful? I'm sick of hearing that word!"

"I guess that's possible in your case," I say dryly. "I've never had the opportunity to hear too much of it."

"Don't be so stupid," says Helen. "It doesn't make people love you more. It just confuses them about what they really think of you."

In a minute Imogene's going to come out of the bathroom, and I don't want to be here when she does. "I'm going to bed," I say wearily. "Tell Imogene it's all right. I don't want any part of Daniel."

Brave words. When I think of him singing "Riding in My Car" to me that day before Imogene came barging in, when I think of him singing "Sittin' on the Dock of the Bay" at the lake before Imogene hit me in the head with the Frisbee . . . I sigh deeply, trudge up the stairs to scrape off my green face. There is no "before Imogene." She has been there all the time.

The green comes off, with a rough washcloth and more Vaseline and even a little grease cleaner.

I have been a fool, I tell myself, a fool in a frog suit.

Scrubbed and greasy and exhausted, I lie in my nightgown and look at the sky. It's clouds tonight, not stars. What if Billy is right? That dead quiet feeling has not left me. I remember Dad smiling weakly as he lent me yet another socket wrench. I recall

Aunt Nicole shaking her head and raising her eyebrows in a "What can we do about Daisy?" gesture. Maybe Billy is right. Maybe I should put the car back in the icehouse, give it up. Life seemed much easier before I ever brought the Beetle into the barn.

november

As a child I remember sitting in the car on frozen mornings while my mother turned the key in the ignition and pumped the gas. It wasn't that I was all that anxious to get to school, but anxious for the car itself, and I would rub the armrest tenderly and whisper, "Come on, you good, sweet car, start, and then soon you'll be warm." When the engine finally turned over, I felt it was just as much because of me as Mom. Under the hood there was just rubber and metal, but somehow there was feeling, too. "I'm here," the car seemed to say to me.

If you took apart a person, would it be much different from pistons, pipes, and hoses? Skin, fat, muscle, bone, intestine, liver, heart; even the brain, where it's all supposed to happen, doesn't show much about how it is. A scientific person might tell you that the cerebral cortex is where feelings are generated. How would someone explain the shudder that crawls up my neck when Mr. Fitz walks too close to the back of my chair when I'm working on a tough quiz on the exhaust system? And where does that cold flash come from that rises up for no good reason from my belly button straight up inside my ribs when I think about Billy Hatcher kissing my neck outside the shop-room door? No matter how angry I am with Billy, the thought of that kiss gives me a cold rush.

The point is, you can't take a person's body apart and find the most important part about her, what you call the "heart" but not the actual organ, what you call the soul, what makes the person go, the ideas and feelings, the spirit. So who's to say that a car doesn't have a spirit, too?

Some doctors give up on their patients who they say will never walk again, and then the patients get up their guts and say, "I will, too, walk again," and they do. A mechanic might give up on a car, the way Billy has given up on my Beetle, saying, "That one's a goner, ready for the crusher," or worse, "Sell it for parts." The car can't say, "I am not a goner." But another mechanic can. Another person can.

I try discussing this with Uncle Phil one night when I'm at his house to baby-sit for Arny. Imogene is at Daniel's house, rehearsing. "Can't you always bring a car back to life if you just keep on trying?"

At first he's sort of gentle with me. "Well, honey, sometimes nobody knows what's wrong."

"But," I say, "if you cared enough, couldn't you keep on trying and trying, take it apart piece by piece, fix every single thing, and eventually you'd find what was wrong and start it up?"

"Is that what you're doing with your car?" he asks me, aghast.

I smile. "No. I don't think so, not yet anyway." I check Aunt Nicole, who's got her nose in the phone book, looking up the number of the restaurant they're going to.

Uncle Phil looks thoughtful, cups his chin in his hand, his elbow on his knee, leaning forward, with his feet turned in pigeon-toed. "It can be very complicated. See, there's a harmony that exists in a machine. Sometimes you have to find the exact right balance between parts. They might be working on their own, fixed, I mean, but if they don't work together, it's no go."

Yes. I see what he means, exactly, and I hear my voice getting higher. "Do you mean it's mathematical? You make it sound magical."

Then he remembers that it's me he's talking to. "Cripes," he says. "If you aren't a fifteen-year-old girl . . . No, Daisy, it's not magic. Call it good mechanics. Call it luck."

Aunt Nicole has been silent until now. "Oh, Phil." She speaks softly. "You know there isn't any such thing as luck."

I think if they just would consider that there might be something behind the science, a force, a god, something that creates things and works with the things people create, something making the world happen—all the parts working in harmony, like music, like a play, the air and the tides and the orbiting planets and the hearts and pistons—if they would allow for this possibility, then they'd understand their own sciences much better. But what do I know? I've still got an old Beetle in the barn that won't go, and for math or magic, I'm none the wiser.

"Ask your dad to have a look," Uncle Phil pleads.

"I can't," I tell him, with a frown at Aunt Nicole that's meant to discourage her from offering her own services again.

"Daisy—" she begins.

"Aunt Nick, let me keep trying for a while," I beg. I'd do anything to keep them all out of the barn, especially Dad. If they discuss this conversation with him—

"All your hard work!" Aunt Nicole grieves. I clench my teeth against her sympathy.

"Wouldn't you want the same?" I appeal.

"Me? Oh, Daisy, if I had done at your age what you have done, I can only think of where I would be now." There's a warm spot inside my chest: Aunt Nicole is proud of me!

"A little while longer," I say. "After the play." I listen to myself in dismay, hearing how I've begun to put off looking again at my car. I'm afraid of what I'll find if I look. I'm afraid I'll never find that glitch on my own.

I am so busy, though, in the next few weeks, chasing down gels for lights and climbing ladders to make last-minute adjustments, planning curtain cues with Ben, and practicing lighting cues with Billy.

I guess you could say Billy and I have assumed a working relationship. He comes over one Saturday when his brother is home, drives the black Thunderbird right into the barn, and makes me help him change the oil. We work with the door open to the cold wind. The Beetle sits there, silenced, and Billy never even glances toward it if he thinks I'm watching.

At one point he looks me in the eye and says, "I'm sorry for what I said about your car. I meant it, but I can't blame you for trying." He turns away.

He's so honest that I have to laugh, but just for a moment, because what I want to do is lean my head against Billy's dark blue sweatshirt back and cry over my poor, dead Beetle. But I see something else, too: that Billy tried to hurt me because he cared about me and thought I didn't care back, not in the same way. But now I could never say that I don't care about Billy. Two months ago he was just some senior guy in a good car, but now he's practically everywhere. I suppose we'll have to keep things friendly for a few more weeks, until the play closes at the end of November. Then I'll only have to see him in auto shop.

Still, I can't recall through any part of me the anger I felt toward him on Halloween night. Although I push him to the back of my mind—him and my Beetle—I keep him there and don't try to push him completely out. In the back of my mind he is a dark blue sweatshirt, shadowed eyes, a warmth, a kindness.

There's a car show at the airfield Saturday, and Mr. Fitz has assigned us all to go.

"You people who have cars, find someone who doesn't," he directs. "Get out there and see some engines, have some conversations. A good mechanic has a lot to learn from other mechanics."

It's okay. Dad or Uncle Phil will take me. I look down and open my notebook as if trying to find something.

"Daisy?" Ben taps my arm. "Want a ride with me and Bill?" I look across Ben to see Billy watching expectantly.

"Ben thinks he can bum his mother's car," says Billy. "We'll pick you up at nine."

Saturday morning I pull on my jeans and a yellow shirt. I gulp down a bowl of Cheerios and run out to the barn for the purple New York University sweatshirt I left in the Beetle's backseat one warm afternoon.

I pat the Beetle's hood, reassuring it. "I'll be back later," I whisper. "Got to go see some other engines so I can learn to take care of you better." I glance around, feeling as if I'm skipping out of chores for the day. Tires crunch the gravel of the driveway, and I dash out to meet Ben and Billy. But only Billy is there, in the black Thunderbird.

"Hi. Where's Ben?"

Billy leans across the passenger seat and opens the door. "Baby-sitting," he answers. "His mother's got the flu, so Ben has to watch his little sisters." Oh. Ben used to call Imogene and get his sisters together with Arny. Too bad he won't do that today.

I feel oddly aloof and grown up, riding along in the morning chill on the shiny vinyl cushions of Billy Hatcher's famed Thunderbird. Billy looks like a Thunderbird himself, with his cowlicky, almost black hair, thin face, and beaky nose. What am I doing alone with him, a senior boy, in his car? I suppose it would seem more ordinary if Ben were along.

As if reading my thoughts, Billy says, "I hope you don't mind going just with me, Daisy. I figured you'd need to go anyway."

I feel guilty and wistful, wishing Billy didn't think he had to apologize for being alone with me. "It's okay. My father will probably be going later, so he can give me a ride home if you need to leave or anything."

"That's all right," he says. "I always find plenty to study at these things."

"Study?" I say. "That's what I need to do, all right."

"Are you making any progress?" he asks politely.

"Oh, yes," I lie. "There's just a long way to go yet. I'll get it all done, eventually, and maybe by then I'll be sixteen and have my license."

Something bugs him about that. "Sure, if they don't send you up the river first for driving underage," he says.

"Oh, you must be a fine citizen, Billy," I retort. "I suppose you always do the exact speed limit?"

"As a matter of fact, I do," he says, then shrugs one shoulder, "most of the time." He grins at me, shaking off the moment, and turns onto the airport road, a bumpy tree-lined lane that opens out onto a spacious, concrete airfield. It is all sky, and pavement, and grass between the landing strips, and a control tower stuck plop in the middle that looks as if it could be made of Lego bricks. Behind it wait rows of delicate white and yellow airplanes and one sleek private jet. The parking lots and lawns are packed with cars on display: older models, including some I recognize from Summer Cruises, jacked-up trucks and funny cars, racing models (I think I spot Uncle Phil's red Mazda cap bobbing among them), and over there a few Beetles, VW buses, and Porsches. Something about their beautiful shapes on that wide field makes a little ache in my heart, and I can't be mad at Billy anymore, not with all this. Who else could I like being here with as much as him? Suddenly I look over at Billy, standing with his hands in his pockets and his head up, looking at everything, and I tell myself: We're here together. Together, we're here.

Billy and I walk along between the cars, examining engines. Billy seems fascinated with the souped-up Chevys and Ford pickup trucks and is especially taken with one long white Thunderbird. He stalks along in his black sneakers, making little remarks to me: "Look at those sidewalls. Gorgeous!" He hunkers down in his jeans to peer inside an engine, slides an itchy finger along a big Chrysler tail fin. We pause to watch a demonstration of an unoiled engine blowing all by itself, on a block, pistons shooting off and smoke rising for the grand finale.

"Oil's well that ends well," I say as we walk away.

"Stop it." Billy rolls his eyes and chuckles, puts one hand on my shoulder. "Why are you here, Daisy? Where did you come from?"

I laugh with him, happy to be here. "Pluto, the dark planet. Come and I'll show you a beautiful overhead cam." I grab his arm and haul him over to an early Porsche Carrera. "See the angle of the cams? It's ingenious."

"Why?" asks Billy.

"Powerful, that's why."

He smirks. "I'm beginning to wonder about your upbringing, Daisy Pandolfi."

"Why?" It's my turn to ask. "Would it bother you one bit if I were a boy?"

He shrugs his shoulder again. "Sorry. I didn't mean it to sound that way. Anyhow, if I were a girl, would you automatically assume that I speed unlawfully in my T-Bird?"

"Not if you were Helen," I say. "Maybe if you were Imogene."

"Well, Imogene . . ." he begins.

"Watch it," I say, as Uncle Phil's red cap looms near. Dad appears beside him. And I'm happier to see them than I've been in weeks, because I have Billy to introduce to them.

"Daisy, kid." My father greets me. "Are you going to be everywhere from now on?"

I lean on him to make him shut up. "Hi, Unk," I say, and introduce them both to Billy.

"Billy Hatcher?" Uncle Phil asks. "Of the mean black Thunderbird?" You see why I've grown up associating people with their cars. "Want to see a racer?" he offers. "Stop by." They head off in the direction of the food trucks.

"Time for lunch?" says Billy. We buy hamburgers and sodas and walk toward a sunny open spot beside the airfield.

"That's Imogene's father?" asks Billy. "She's got

his looks, but . . ." He twists his mouth, lost for words.

"Not his style?" I supply. I surprise myself by saying, "She's all right, really." I'm a fake, a fake in a great mood.

"No, Daisy, don't get me wrong. Imogene's a nice girl. I just don't picture her growing up around race-tracks."

"Well, she did. We all did. She just didn't hang around the pit the way I did. I didn't always, either. Sometimes we all sat in the grass and made daisy chains."

He dips his french fry in my ketchup and smiles at me. We sit dunking our fries and sipping sodas, and waving away little yellow jacket bees. Summer is long since over, but on an Indian summer day like this it hardly seems possible that there could come to be a need for sweaters and mittens and antifreeze. I finish my fries and lean back on my elbows, eyes closed to the sun.

"I think you have a prejudice against American cars," Billy accuses me. "I couldn't get you interested in any of them. The only things that caught your eye were European motors."

"You know what I'd like?" I say. "One of those old, big Ford pickups, with the running board and the fat fenders. Red. Or shiny black."

"With a puppy in the back," teases Billy.

"A Dalmatian."

"To match the truck?"

"Of course."

Billy lies on his back with his eyes closed, sunning himself.

"My family's not like your family, all hanging around together and helping each other out," he says after a long time.

"Chewing each other out, more like," I say.

"That's just part of it," says Billy. "You're all in it together."

"Yes, and it can get pretty cramped. You don't know. I can't do anything without getting pestered, questioned, spied on—" I'm not being fair. I'm the one being evasive; they're not trying too hard to spy.

"They care," says Billy. He sits up with his knees up in front of him and his elbows resting on his knees, his bony scrubbed hands hanging down in front of his knees.

"Oh, yes, they definitely care," I say sarcastically, "whether you want them to or not, whether it's their business or not!" They think it *is* their business. That's just the trouble.

Billy shakes his head and leans it on his arms and talks looking down into his lap.

"You're lucky," he says. "And you can't even see it."

"My father and my aunt and uncle—they're all trying to second-guess the work I'm doing on the car."

"They're protecting you! They care about you."

"Well, everybody's parents care about them!" I blurt the statement without thinking, and Billy stands up and walks away. He goes to the edge of the grass and stands there with the toes of his high-tops hanging over onto the tarmac of the parking lot.

I get up and stand beside him. Then I say another

stupid thing. "Mr. Fitz cares, Billy."

He laughs. "Yes, he does," he says. "But he says the same thing to me that he says to all the seniors. Maybe not out loud, but inside."

"Go forth into the universe." I quote Mr. Fitz.

Billy's arm sweeps across the sky as though he were taking off, sign language for what he thinks.

"Isn't that what parents should say?" I ask.

He turns and looks at me. "Parents should be like yours," he says, as if I were his child, not theirs.

I cross my arms to keep the space between us. He puts his hands on my shoulders, there on the grass of the airfield.

"I'm the youngest, you know," he says, starting a story I'm afraid to hear. "My parents put up with each other until I graduated from eighth grade." He's staring straight ahead at the little parked airplanes, and I watch his face out of the corner of my eye. "My father made me put all my graduation money right in the bank. He said I'd need the money." He rolls his eyes a little, laughing a not-funny laugh. His hands stroke up and down my arms. "So it's been just the three of us—me and Joe and Mom—since I've been in high school. Mom keeps on at the garden center, and Dad's out in Ohio, still trying to be a writer. He was sending money for a while."

Billy goes on, and now he puts his arms all the way around me. "On my birthday—last April—Dad called me up. He said I was a man now, and I could work to support myself." Billy's hands are stroking my hair, his fingers playing along the woven strands of my braid. His touch clouds my thinking.

I place my hands firmly on his back; his red shirt under them is so clean and dry, his back under the shirt so hard and straight. I say into his ear, "So now . . . ?"

"So now I'm on my own. This is my last show because I'll have to work. I'm going to finish *The King and I*—Mom insisted—and then I'll be doing overtime through Christmas, working Christmas trees."

"At the place where your mom works?"

"Yeah. It's easy, because Mom can drive. After Christmas I'm going to have to find something else, work out transportation, the whole thing." Billy is all business now, looking over my head and plotting.

I can think better if he lets go of me, so I twist away and squat down, zipping up my backpack.

He looks down at me, his hands hanging at his sides. "Joe's got to sell the T-Bird," he says. "This might be the last weekend I'll have it."

I can't begin to measure his sadness.

"You'll have to get your own car," I say stupidly.

Billy makes that laughing sound again. "There's a mortgage to pay," he says. "And Joe needs college tuition. And me, I wanted to go to tech school at least, or college. But now I don't know. I might better just get a job."

Mortgage? Tuition? I get scared just hearing the words. How does Billy feel about it? I stand up at last and look into his face, and my answer is there: raw.

I point to a plane that's about to take off, and together we watch it zoom along the runway and lift into the air. "Flying would be exciting, wouldn't it?" I say.

"Like driving, but different," Billy says. "Faster, and no road underneath you."

"Nothing but air," I add.

Billy laughs, a real laugh this time, and we sit down in the grass again, finish our sodas. Above the airfield the little planes buzz around, taking off and getting ready to land. The air is full of them, like bugs, like gnats, like beetles in the sky.

The play opens the Friday night before Thanksgiving and runs through Sunday night. Dress rehearsal happens Wednesday. They say a bad dress rehearsal makes for a great opening night, but I'll believe it when I see it. This dress rehearsal is a crazy mess of missed cues, flat notes, and forgotten lines. My lights are where they should be, even though the actors all forget to stand on their marks on the stage, so half the time they're standing in the dark.

Miss Ferguson sits in the third row and grows more nervous and cranky as the rehearsal drags on. Helen and the other dancers sit a few rows back, watching until it's their time to go on. It's the first time that Helen has seen many of the scenes, including the one where Anna meets the King of Siam's wives and tells them about her husband, Tom, who died.

The corners of Helen's mouth turn down, and she furtively wipes tears from her eyes. I turn back to ready the spotlight for the Siamese children, who go on next. Helen plays one of the princesses. She gets up to go backstage. At intermission she's nowhere to be found.

"Did you see my sister?" I ask Daniel, who's sitting on the stage apron, studying music and hoping to see but not be seen.

"No. Is something wrong?"

I'm so tired and frazzled that I go ahead and tell him. "She was crying."

"Why?"

"This sappy play!" I blurt, then sing softly, because after all, it's Daniel, who used to seem to understand some things, "Those lines about missing Tom. She does, you know."

"Tom Bixby?"

"No, Tom Thumb," I say sharply, chewing a ragged fingernail. Why does he have to act so dumb? "Tell her I'm looking for her if you see her, please, Daniel," I say stiffly, getting up. He's probably jealous of Bixby for ever having had Helen. Let Imogene have Daniel! I don't need him or want him anywhere around me. Whatever made me think I did?

I don't know where Helen's been hiding, but she's onstage on cue for the second act. She dances the part of Eliza, behind her mask, showing none of her own sadness in her body. It's about the only smooth scene.

After the wretched rehearsal finally ends (eleven-thirty, and I have to be in history at seven fifty-five tomorrow morning), I run around chasing light gels, dump them backstage, and hurry to hear Miss Ferguson's notes. She's not exactly ranting and raving; actually she is remarkably patient with what amounts to a cast of boneheads.

"Anna, find more to do with your hands. Too

much standing around. King, what was wrong with your headpiece?" John Silva makes a face and puts a hand to his head.

"Daniel, watch those flat notes. And, Imogene, don't overdo it!" Daniel and Imogene exchange fed-up looks.

"Actors, get in the right place for your follow spots. And, Daisy, when you're not working that spotlight, get into the wings and stay there." I look up, startled. "Remember, if you can see me—" and the entire cast intones with Miss Ferguson,

"I can see you!"

I blush, but it's not terribly embarrassing because we've done that to practically everyone in the course of the play. In fact, it draws me in. Now I'm really a part of this thing.

Imogene taps me on the shoulder. "Helen had to go," she says. "She asked me to give you a ride home."

"Okay," I say. "Just let me get this stuff put away, and I'll meet you at your car."

"Fifteen minutes," she says.

I'm so tired that I hardly say anything all the way home in the backseat of the Honda. I don't worry that I'm cramping Imogene's style. I sit staring at the back of Daniel's head and wonder, Does he long for a car the way Billy does? Does having a car matter when he lives as close to town—and Imogene—as he does? Our house is four miles out of town, five from school—too far, most cold days, for a bicycle or a skateboard or even a motorbike. Billy's house must be three miles past ours, even more remote.

They take me home first (so they can go off and smooch in Daniel's driveway?), and Daniel gives me his hand to pull me out of the backseat.

"You don't have to do that," I say, embarrassed.

He stands there in the driveway and asks me, "Going to John's party Friday night?" John Silva has invited us all to his house opening night after the show.

"I guess so. You?"

"Everybody's going to be there," says Daniel, and gives me a little wave that's almost a salute. Strange. It's funny Billy didn't mention that party to me. As I walk up the steps, it occurs to me that Billy, up high in his lighting booth, doesn't know too many people in the play besides me and Ben. It's nice being backstage, but it's not the same as being in the cast. We don't share as much as the members of the cast, who have to show off themselves onstage, not their lights or makeup or props. We miss a little of the thrill, but oh, after tonight I can see we still get plenty of stage fright.

Mom and Dad are sitting over coffee at the kitchen table. "Where's Helen?" I ask casually.

"She went to bed."

Upstairs the bathroom door is closed, and a line of light shows underneath. "Let me in," I say, knocking. Helen is sitting on the edge of the bathtub with a bunched-up towel in her lap, and her eyes are red from crying.

"Cut it out," I beg. "Everyone is worried about you."

"Oh, Daisy, I'm beginning to worry myself."

"Why?"

"I thought I was fine, just fine. Then I heard that song tonight." Helen laughs and shakes her head at herself. "Maybe I've just worn myself out dancing. I don't know. Maybe I'm nervous about opening night—and then *Nutcracker* right afterward! I just couldn't stand it tonight. Bixby is everywhere! Now he's even in the play." She sniffs loudly and stands up. I hand her a tissue, and she blows her nose, watching herself in the mirror. "You wouldn't believe how often I hear the name Tom."

"Do you think it would help if you found someone else?" I ask.

"Is that what you think?" Helen demands.

"I haven't the least idea, Helen. Mom mentioned it."

"Well, she's wrong!"

I pause, then put voice to some hard thoughts I've been keeping to myself. "She just wants us both to have boyfriends. I feel like she's sitting waiting for news. And now that you don't have one anymore—" I stop, sure I'm about to say the wrong thing.

Helen studies my face. "No, no," she says. "That's not it at all. She wants us to be happy, that's all."

"Oh, right. To be happy, you have to go in twos. That's what *she* thinks."

"Really? Daisy, can't you see how Mom has been behind you? How she's helped you convince Dad about the Beetle? How she's taken up the slack when you've missed chores? How she's stood back and not even mentioned that she knows your car is completely wrecked?"

"It is not!"

"Yeah, well, she saw it one night over your shoulder. She mentioned it to me but not to Dad."

"She did?"

"Don't be so prickly all the time! What worries Mom, about you and that car—do you want to know?"

Oh, Lord, do I want to know? I make a sort of shrug with my face.

"It's your—it's this wanting something *so much* for yourself. It's the fear that you'll get hurt, as you have. As I have."

We sit there in the bathroom, she on the tub, me on the toilet, just looking at each other.

"Are you lonely, Hel?" I ask.

Tears well up in her eyes again. "Yeah, I am," she admits. "All summer long I had people around me— Bixby and his friends, and softball, and Imogene and Ben were always there. Then Daniel came along, and you . . . Then softball ended. Now Bixby is—well, and Imogene and Daniel are always—" She stops and looks at me nervously and goes on. "And you're always up in the lighting booth or working on your car, and I know it's got problems, Daisy, and I don't blame you, but—" She drops her face in her hands and rubs her eyes, hard. "It's okay," she says, pushing me gently out the bathroom door. "I'll be fine once this blows over."

I stand looking at the closed door for a second.

"What's so great about Tom Bixby anyway?" I yell through the door.

Silence, then: "Imogene is right. You *are* too much, you and that car and—seriously, Daisy—stage crew! You wouldn't know true love if it—if you—just leave me alone!"

I go into my room and shut the door.

During performances everyone working backstage wears black. I don't own one single article of black clothing, so for opening night I borrow a pair of black jeans from my mother and a long black turtleneck tunic from Aunt Nicole.

The school feels odd tonight, the plate glass windows huge and dark with early evening and expectation. My reflection is startling: just face, hair, and hands show, as my black clothes dissolve into the shadows. I stop for a minute and study myself, then pose on one foot and hop down the hall.

"Hey, Daisy in black," says a soft voice from the hallway door. It's Billy, in black, which looks somehow strikingly right with his dark hair and eyebrows. "You're not going to blend into the dark one bit." He's lugging two cube-shaped black boxes with their edges worn away to gray.

"I have something for you," he says so seriously, handing me one of the boxes. I take off the musty lid. Inside rests a velvety black top hat.

"Oh!" I breathe. I try it on, checking my dark reflection in the window.

"And look," says Billy. He opens the other box and pulls out a black satin pancake, gives it a whack against his knee, and snaps the top hat onto his own head.

"They were my grandfather's," he explains. "I figured, here we are in backstage black." He turns to the window and cups his hands around his eyes to peer through the glass to the parking lot outside.

"People are beginning to come," I say. "I'd better get backstage."

Billy turns suddenly and takes my face in his hands. At his touch I feel a cool fluttering in my stomach, which surprises me into looking into his eyes. There is a tenderness there that reminds me in a way of Helen's look when I tell her to stop trying to paint makeup all over me. He turns my face sideways, kisses me sweetly on my earlobe, and smiles into my eyes. Suddenly the moment is gone as he gives me a loud smooch, right into my ear.

I yowl and jump back, expecting a joke, but his face still wears that tender look.

"Break a leg, Daisy," he says quietly. "Remember, if you can see me—"

Together we finish, "I can see you."

With a thump of the big double doors he is gone to his lighting booth.

In the wings of the stage I sit on my stool beside my follow spotlight and manage not to get the jitters, not badly much anyway. Ben, the stage manager, gives me a hug, and says, "Break a leg," before he hurries to his post at the curtain.

In no time it's curtain time. The sliver of houselight visible under the curtain dims. Ben's back muscles clench as he pulls the heavy rope to raise the curtain. Two spots of sweat have already appeared in the black armpits of his T-shirt. There comes a fabulous, itchy moment as the audience hushes and the stage lights fade up to reveal Anna and Louis and some sailors in their ship sailing down the river toward Bangkok. My follow spot picks up the royal messenger, as he makes his stilted welcome speech and executes a grand bow, made silly by his flopping pointy hat. The audience chuckles, just where it's supposed to, and we're off.

When the stage lights go down and the house-lights come up for intermission, my hands are finally empty. I reach up to touch my earlobe, and find it satiny soft around my hard gold earring. Never mind, dopey Daisy, I tell myself, he kissed you so fast he never had a chance to notice. Then again, maybe he did.

At intermission I run into Helen in her bright blue leotard. "Come here!" She grips my elbow and pulls me into the locker room, pulls a plastic bag out of her ballet satchel. Inside is a pair of black satin pumps.

"What?" I ask. "Aren't these Mom's?"

"Now, look," Helen says. "Everyone is dressing up for John's party as if it were a real opening night on Broadway. Wait till you see what Imogene's wearing."

"I—"

"I know. You didn't know. And what would you have worn if you had known, Daisy?" She's right. She's always telling me to get something glamorous, just in case. Instead all I have that's the least bit dressy are church dresses—not for opening night.

"And don't try to tell me that you don't care, because you will."

"Well, I—"

"You won't believe me, Daze, but you look gorgeous in what you're wearing, just those black things. Mom must have known you would."

"This is her idea?" My mom? In her jeans and clogs, dreaming up an opening night do for me?

"She saw you come home last Saturday with Billy. Is he where you got that hat?"

"Listen, Helen, what makes you think you know everything?"

"Tell me that I'm wrong, then, Daisy Pandolfi."

I can't think of a thing to say.

"Mom sent you her shoes and her rhinestone earrings."

"Come on! I'm not the rhinestone type, Helen."

"Oh, shut up, Daisy. Just shut up for once."

I shock her by saying meekly, "Okay, Helen."

"Okay? Okay!" She pats my head. "Good girl! I'll meet you backstage. Break a leg, Daisy."

"Break your own stupid leg, Helen," I tell her.

From my spot in the shadowy wings I spy on the audience as they file back into their seats. Bixby! I wonder whose idea it was for him to come to the play. In the second act you don't see Helen's face at all; it stays hidden behind her Eliza mask. I wonder if she'll notice Bixby, outside the aura of the stage lights?

The second act is Imogene's time to shine. She and Daniel, as a slave girl and her boyfriend, try to elope and get caught. There are a few desperate, wonderful songs. I have to hand it to them: They're good, those two, good on their own and good together.

The curtain falls at last. Backstage erupts in cheers and howls that the audience can hear perfectly clearly.

Feeling left out, I make my way through to my family. Everyone is congratulating Uncle Phil and Aunt Nicole on Imogene's wonderful singing.

"Daisy!" my dad greets me. "Wonderful lights."

"Did you have fun, babe?" Mom asks.

"Whew!" I answer with a big grin.

"Helen's backstage?" asks Dad.

"The cast can't come out, just us impostors," I tell him.

"You're going to the party, though, aren't you?" asks Mom.

"Yeah," I say sheepishly. "Thanks for the shoes." I swing the bag by its string handle. Mom and I find other things to look at besides each other.

Dad, puzzled, says, "What shoes?"

"Just some shoes I needed," I tell him. "No big deal."

He shrugs his shoulders, left out. "The hat's great," he says, and I give it a little tap.

"Thanks," I say. "Well, I—" I look around the auditorium, which is already almost empty. Up by the lighting booth Billy sits with his feet up on the chair in front of him and his top hat in his lap.

"Go ahead," says Mom. "We'll see you in the morning."

"Sleep late tomorrow," says Dad. "You need it."

I stand in front of Billy, my top hat in one hand and the bag of shoes in the other. "What are you doing here?" I ask.

"Just basking in the glow of the stage," he says seriously.

"It was good, wasn't it?"

He smiles, looking down at the matching hat in his hands. "Daisy," he says, "you'd better avoid lonesome hallways."

"How's that?" I smile.

"Something comes over me," he tells me, his eyes guarded.

"Oh," is all I can say, but something bends inside me. I smile at him, then look away quickly. I want to take his hat and put it back on his head, jolly like it was before.

"I'm glad it's all right," he says. "I'm not going to John's."

"Why not?" He just shrugs and continues to look at the stage. I'm suddenly angry because I realize that Billy doesn't want to be at the party with everyone celebrating when it's his last show. And I'm angry because I'm standing here with Mom's high-heeled shoes and rhinestone earrings, and now I'm not going to bother wearing them, even though Helen will be mad.

"Fine," I say, and I walk away, swinging my bag by its string. I don't feel like going, either, I tell myself. Nothing to do with Billy. I'm just let down now that the glow of opening night is passed. I won't show him how much I wish he were coming, how left out I'm going to feel with all the performers having their celebration. When I get to the door, I turn and sweep a grand bow, taking off Billy's grandfather's top hat. I leave it on the first seat of the front row and go out the door.

The play is over on Sunday, and we strike the set, knocking it down as fast as possible, prying at seams and cracking joints with crowbars and hammers. We need to be quick, Miss Ferguson orders, to clear the auditorium for the Christmas concert. Our speed makes us wild and violent. Our exhaustion makes us careless, and Ben drops a two-pound hammer on his toe. Tears spring to his eyes. He sits down with a thud and, scowling, watches Imogene and Daniel wrestle a plank into the backstage storage room. Helen is gone tonight; for weeks her rehearsals for *The Nutcracker* have overlapped with our show, and now she is free to leave. The Sugarplum Fairy doesn't risk life and limb striking sets.

Billy's not here, either. "They're already starting with Christmas trees at Hendries'," he told me in auto shop, when he asked me to come for both of us. "People come and tag their trees, and I have to help them."

I agreed to take the lights back to Sister Grace, and Ben and I have been carting lights to Imogene's car all evening. It seems light-years since Billy and I first brought the lights from St. Mary's. "So how's your good old Beetle?" Ben asks, either to be nice or to keep his mind off Imogene and Daniel.

"Still in the barn," I say, trying to sound chipper. With my car nothing has changed through the entire play.

"Dead or alive?"

"Mostly dead." I sigh. To change the subject, I ask, "Are you okay?"

"Sure," he says. "I have eight other toes."

"That's not what I meant." I meet his eyes.

Ben puffs a breath that sends his front hair flying up. "Stupid old Imogene," he says tenderly. "And stupid me for caring."

"She can't help it," I tell him.

"No," he says then. "Neither can Daniel." For once the mention of Daniel's name doesn't cause me to blush.

It's the Friday night after Thanksgiving. Helen and I have spent the afternoon making spaghetti sauce with pork and garlic, and now we're attempting to make our own pizza dough. Arny is making a neat sort of mess with the cheese grater and a mushy lump of mozzarella. Uncle Phil and Dad are in the living room, sorting through all the newspapers and tying them up for recycling. That's what they say they're doing anyway. Really Uncle Phil is going through every paper reading the political cartoons and *Calvin and Hobbes* and Dad is flipping pages and tearing out anything he should have read but didn't. I wonder if they ever sat dreaming over the "Repairables" as Billy does, or did things come easily to them, too, when they were kids?

"Look here," Uncle Phil says. "Stewart Jones."

"Stewart who? Oh, yeah, the Jaguar guy? What's he doing in there?"

"The usual. Pretty outstanding."

"What Jaguar guy?" I ask. I'm trying to pound my dough into a circle, but it looks more like a cock-eyed square.

"This is impossible!" says Helen. Her dough looks like a triangle.

"He's a blind mechanic," Uncle Phil says. "Fixes old Jags. He had one down at The Landing last year, on a trailer for the Cruise. Pretty bizarre." He says it *bee-zar*.

"What's so bizarre about it?" Helen asks. "Blind people can do anything."

"He doesn't drive, does he?" I ask. There's a hole in the middle of my dough, and I'm trying to patch it with a piece cut from the edge.

"No more than you do, Daze," my father says, making Helen's eyebrows go up. "How could he be a mechanic if he didn't?"

Arny says, "He's a mechanic without eyes?"

"He's got eyes, honey," says Uncle Phil. "They don't work, though."

Dad is reading the article. "Says he can find things other people miss. He can listen to an engine, stand back, and say, 'You've got a loose rocker arm there.'"

I squash my lousy pizza dough back into a ball and close my eyes as I knead it. It's like a puffy bubble, bouncy as rubber bands and tough as a new fan belt. I get physical with it, my eyes squeezed shut, slamming it on the counter into what feels like a circle. I punch my fist into the middle to press the air out, and feel my circle get wider. "Hey, try this!" I tell Helen. We stand there making pizza with our eyes shut. It goes fine until she gets the wise idea of tossing it up in the air. Arny lunges and catches it before it hits the floor. We press it with our fingers onto cookie sheets, and Arny spoons sauce and sprinkles cheese on the top. He's got a much finer touch in the kitchen than Helen or I ever will.

By the time Mom and Aunt Nicole come home from shopping, the pizza's ready, and a salad, too. Dad and Uncle Phil pile the tied-up newspapers by the back door, and we all sit down to eat.

"Where's Imogene tonight?" Mom asks, looking around suddenly.

"She's in Westport," says Helen. "Daniel is playing his guitar at a coffeehouse."

"How nice!" Mom says.

"I guess you could play the guitar blind," Arny says, still thinking about Stewart Jones. Yes, I think, and I wonder if Imogene would have done so well with Daniel if he were blind.

Feeling lonesome, I pull on an old ski sweater of Dad's and go out to the barn after dinner. In my good-luck red high-tops I press the Beetle's pedals, turn the key, and start her up, giving myself only an instant to wonder whether I've lost my mind.

It's the worst thing I've ever heard: no oil, and then the most hellish awful crunching noise. I shut the engine off immediately and go for a can of oil. Just a little, a little at a time. I turn the key again and listen, listen, listen. What would a blind man hear? The little engine sounds old, injured, abused, and my chest hurts with the guilt that's welling up there.

It would help if I knew precisely what my engine

sounded like healthy, every part, and could divide the sound into sections or functions through just listening, as that blind mechanic must. But I can't. I open my eyes and look, and that's no better than it ever has been. All I can see is the outside of the engine, after all, and there's nothing wrong there. But inside, somewhere inside, that's where it all goes wrong.

I stand there with my head in my arms, leaning on the roof of the car, my hair falling across its dusty purple skin, and it's all I can do not to cry. It's cold in the barn, and I'm frozen inside, too, but there is a heat of tears behind my eyes that won't be iced down. I insist. I force myself silent. I force myself to think of what I can do, whom I can go to, how I can move now. Would Stewart Jones come listen to my engine? No, he's a Jaguar man. There couldn't be anything more different, could there? Dennis Schweitzer is the Beetle expert, he's the man to call in for a listen, but how can I get him over here without having to deal with Dad? Maybe I should take the engine out, get it up on blocks like Mr. Schweitzer's, and—

And that's when I hear the dripping. Just one drop, then another, two drops plinking dully under my car.

I hit the floor as though I've been shot and shove myself on my stomach under the rear of my car. With my fingers, I search the barn floor for the oil, watching carefully to see which part of the engine I'm under. But it's just dirt, packed barn dust and ancient straw, cigarette ash and pebbles from the driveway. No oil.

Puzzled, I lie still, and above my head in the dark

I hear another drip. And another. They don't sound like *drip* down here. They say *plink, plunk*. They're not falling on dirt; they're falling on metal, somewhere above me, somewhere inside my engine.

I drag myself out on my stomach. There's brown dirt all over the front of Dad's gray sweater. I twist my hair into a rope and tuck it inside the sweater's neck. I lie down on my back and push myself backward under the car. *Plink. Plunk.* No drops fall onto my face, my hands.

Oil is leaking inside my engine. I close my eyes and listen, and move my head until I'm right beneath the pipe where the oil is slowly falling. It falls in one spot, right above my ear, two drops at a time. It must be a little hole, then, not a crack. It hits hard, as though it has dripped from a height. Well, I already know it's not on the bottom of the crankcase; I've gone over that a hundred times. It must be on the side, as high as—on a level with—the pistons. Nothing to do with rocker arms. No. Whole inches away from them.

As I pull myself out from under and stand up, I can't dust myself off for trying to keep all the tears from falling from my eyes. I give up. I give up, I really do. I stagger into the house like a dirty zombie and collapse into a chair. My father and his brother and my mother are sitting over coffee and leftover pumpkin pie. Aunt Nick and Arny are doing the dishes, and Helen has the TV on in the living room.

I may as well just make an announcement. "I've got a hole in my crankcase!" I bellow, and burst into sobs, shedding dirt and leaves all over the table and floor. If Daniel were here, he'd say I was becoming one with my vehicle, so it's a good thing he's not. Arny comes and throws his arms around me, water, dish towel, and all.

"Good grief!"

"How on God's good earth—"

"That blessed valve job! You silly ignoramus!"

The grown-ups are all yelling at once, over my crying head, until Helen's calm voice breaks through from the doorway.

"So, do you suddenly want help or something?" She's like a judge, completely neutral and uncaring. She's holding the remote control in one hand and a toe shoe with a needle and thread dangling from it in the other.

I look up at her stern face and say, "No, just sympathy."

Aunt Nicole laughs, and my mother stands up and holds my head against her stomach. Dad and Uncle Phil are staring at each other like blond and gray bookends with no books in between, talking to each other with their eyes, arguing silently.

But before they reach a decision, I reach one on my own. "I do want help," I say quietly, trying to keep my voice from quavering. "If Billy Hatcher can come over, would someone go pick him up?"

"Billy who?" says Aunt Nicole.

"Doesn't know any more than *you* do," says my father.

"The kid from the show at the airfield?" guesses Uncle Phil.

"He's as good as I am, and he'll help me and not take over," I declare.

"I'll go get him," says Helen, more to get out of the room than anything else, I think.

"Helen—" Mom begins.

"Please," I say. "If I can just find the problem, then I think I can fix it."

"You *think*?" says Mom.

"I bet," I say.

Uncle Phil snorts. "You selling chances now?"

Dad is making noises, not words. He sighs and sputters and blows out his cheeks.

But Aunt Nicole says firmly, "I'll put my money on Daisy."

I've never called Billy's house before. I've always just counted on running into him at shop, in the hall, at the theater. It makes me think for a minute. Now that he's going to be doing Christmas trees all through Christmas and then who knows what after, am I ever going to see him?

"Billy?"

"Yes?" Does he know it's me? I sigh, tongue-tied. It's all too much, the car and him and everything. "Daisy? Is something wrong?"

"Boy, is there," I say. "Billy, I've got a Repairable."

"Oh," he says. "*Now* you tell me."

"Billy, don't be like that," I say, fed up with his prickly poor-me attitude, his attitude that says you-can't-help-me and you-don't-care. I do, and maybe I can.

"Billy, don't *be* like that," he mimics.

"Will you come over? Helen says she'll come get you."

"Are you sure you don't want me to fly?" he asks. "You know, now that I've got wings and a halo and all."

But it's me who's acting angelic, not him. "I'm just offering," I say.

"I accept," he says, and hangs up the phone.

"You need some cows to warm up this barn," Billy tells me.

"So I've been told." I sigh, thinking of Daniel.

"Cows and horses and pigs," says Billy. "And on Christmas Eve they'd all talk."

Has he gone giddy or something just because I've invited him over?

"Really," he says. "After midnight, when everybody's sleeping."

"We're never here," I say. "We go to midnight mass Christmas Eve." Can we get to the subject of the car? I'd like to say.

"Oh, so do we. But I wouldn't if I had cows. I'd sneak in, so I could hear them talk."

"No cows," I answer. "Just plenty of cars."

"That's true. And one almost dead." Now we're getting down to it.

"Alive!" I retort. "She lives."

He lifts one hand in a gesture of peace.

I toss him a socket wrench, and together we drop down under the Beetle. "Now, remember," I say. "We were just driving along, and something went bump."

"And there was oil everywhere, you said, right?"

"How's that?" asks Billy, raising one eyebrow, seeing my face now.

"They worked magic for my mother—they and this Beetle, together." I lay my hand gently on the running board. The floor is cold and damp, and I feel a shiver starting low on my spine. Now that I know what's wrong, I can get to work and fix it.

"What kind of magic?" Billy asks seriously.

"It made her fall in love with my father," I tell him quietly. "I thought it would help me keep the car alive."

"It's not dead, you know," says Billy.

"Looks it," I answer. My teeth begin to chatter from cold and fear.

"Are you cold, Daisy?" he asks. "Get in the car." He opens the passenger door and ushers me into the backseat, then climbs in beside me. From the well he pulls the maroon-and-white football blanket that my mother knitted when my father was at Cornell. He wraps it over my knees.

"Do you know what's the trouble with you, Daisy." It's not a question.

"Tell." I sigh deeply and begin to relax a little under the warm blanket.

"You know all about what goes on in a car's engine."

"Obviously not all," I say sarcastically.

"You know all the parts, what goes where," Billy continues. "But you don't know what goes on inside a car."

"In the engine?"

"No. Inside a car." He rests his arm on the back

of the seat and strokes my hair, which is probably full of dust from the barn floor.

I shudder and begin to feel tears coming at last from wherever they've been hiding. "If you're nice to me, Billy Hatcher, I'm going to cry," I whisper.

"I'm not ever going to be nice to you," Billy says, bringing his arm around my shoulder.

"I'm going to have to rebuild that whole valve," I tell him.

He laughs. "Yeah. It's repairable, somehow."

I smile. Somehow, knowing I've got a big problem has helped him forget his own. He's right. Inside the car, in the driver's seat, or in the well, or in the backseat, where I've never been (because I was too little or too big?), live different kinds of magic.

"Whatever you do, Hatcher, don't kiss me," I tell him.

But he goes ahead and kisses me anyway.

december

Dad can't possibly take my news well.

"You sucked a valve?"

I nod my head, swallow, and force myself to hold my father's glance. With a sharp twist of his head, he turns away from me and stands up. He says a bad word and paces the kitchen. He reaches to the top of the refrigerator behind the old radio and pulls out a package of cigarettes I didn't know was hidden there.

He lights one and paces toward the window over the sink, glaring out at the barn and the bright, thin, almost-winter sunlight. He scuffs a loafer on the floor, swearing again, and I sit silently, waiting for the storm.

When it comes, it comes with a low rumble. He doesn't tell me how long he's had the Beetle, how long it's been in the family, how much it means to him and Mom and Uncle Phil and Aunt Nicole, to all of us.

He says, "That crankcase is going to be hard to replace." He says it as if he's telling me that he's in mortal pain.

I say, "Do you mean hard, difficult? Or hard, expensive?"

"Both!" He puffs the cigarette, then takes a look at it and throws it in the sink. It sizzles for a second and goes out. "Just how do you suppose—"

"Christmas," I say. "I don't want any presents at all. I don't need clothes or anything else. I don't want any necklaces or music or stuff. And I'm going to start working. I'm almost old enough, and Aunt Nicole's been asking me if I'd start. Not just oil changes, real stuff. Anyway, I think I can convince her." My voice runs down as I get to the end of my short list of ideas.

"And it has to happen right away, I suppose?" Dad says.

"It *has* to get fixed right away," I say low. "Dad, it's been dead out there for two months almost. I'd only just got it going when the valve went. I worked all summer long on it, Dad, all summer long! I couldn't just give it over to you the first time I had a problem."

"The problem could have been avoided," my father roars.

"But only if I asked for help!" I holler back.

"Well, what do you think you're asking for *now*?"

My eyes are wet more with concentration than misery. I look at my hands on the tabletop and realize that there's no lump in my throat, no sobs coming up.

"This is a negotiation," I tell my father in Helen's judge voice. "Not a plea."

He strides across the kitchen to the refrigerator and slaps the cigarette pack into its hiding place behind the radio. He stands with his back to me then, and I sit wondering which way he'll go.

"I didn't expect you to plead," he says finally. He's wearing a yellow broadcloth shirt hanging loose outside his old plaid pants, and he shudders a little in the middle of his back, between his shoulder blades.

It's my turn to rumble. "I'm not just going to give it over!" I shout. "I made a mistake, a really stupid mistake. Okay?"

"Which could have been avoided if you'd just let someone else take a look at the thing." He waves his arm to include the whole world (all the adult mechanics who are better than I am) and flings his hand toward the barn door. Then he raises one finger and walks across the kitchen toward me. "Well, I'm going to take a look at it now, Daisy girl." His brown eyes are intent on mine.

"Okay," I say. "But I'm going to do all the work."

He slams his hand down on the table beside me so hard I jump up from my chair. At the back door I stop, my hand on the knob for support. "If you would come and look over my shoulder . . ." I begin.

"What, and watch you make more lousy screwups?" My father gapes at me. "And not say a word, I suppose?"

I suck my bottom lip.

"Daisy," he says, "there's so much trouble I could save you. I've already done all the stupid things you can do to a car."

"You've sucked a valve?"

"No, but I've driven on a tire until I crushed the rim. I've wrecked a whole transmission. I've blown a hole in a muffler, just fooling around."

I'm leaning forward with my hand on the end of the counter. "Really?"

"Look, everything that hasn't happened to me? It's because I learned how to keep it from happening. I could have—" He walks over to me and rests his hand on the top of my head, pushes my head around in a circle. "Isn't there anything I can say to you about that Beetle?"

I shake my head. Then it comes to me. "Don't tell me what to do. Just tell me when I go wrong."

Dad stares at the space over my head. "Less wear and tear on the car that way," he says.

"That's the important thing," I whisper. I turn the knob and go outside.

"So where do I buy a crankcase?" Mom asks Helen and me. "Do you think Fox sells them?" It's Saturday morning, the second weekend of December, and Mom and Helen are going Christmas shopping in Hartford.

"That's right, Mom," Helen says. "Right behind the pillowcases."

Fox is the department store where Mom usually buys our Christmas presents, there and a little shop in Kent that has beautiful handmade sweaters and embroidered blouses. This is the first time either of us has asked for anything automotive. I have a feeling it won't be the last.

"Crankcase. Piston rod. Maybe a whole piston.

And that whole valve assembly . . ." I'd like to faint to the floor, but instead I lay my head on the kitchen table and run my hands through my hair.

"Among others. I was thinking." Dad looks away, out the kitchen window toward the icehouse. "You should ask Dennis Schweitzer to find you a crankcase."

"You want me to do that?" I am amazed.

"It was your uncle's idea, actually," Dad admits. "He's gotten friendly with Schweitzer lately." Well, I guess that's a good thing for Imogene and Daniel.

"Let's ask him," I agree.

Dad drives us over to the Schweitzers' in the Porsche.

Imogene, wide-eyed, opens the condominium door.

"I thought I heard that thing," she says, waving a hand toward the Porsche.

"Daisy! Mr. Pandolfi." Daniel appears behind Imogene and ushers us inside. A fire is lit in the fireplace. The guitar lies sprawled across the couch, and sheet music is strewn about. I envision Daniel and Imogene sitting there singing together, warmed by the fire.

Mr. Schweitzer comes in from the garage, wiping his fingers on a rag.

"Hello, Daisy," he says slowly, and extends a hand to Dad. "Dennis Schweitzer," he says.

"This is my father, Mr. Schweitzer." I introduce them.

"John Pandolfi," says Dad. They shake hands warily.

"You've helped Daisy with her car," Dad states. "I appreciate that."

"Daisy's a good mechanic," Mr. Schweitzer replies.

"Yes," says Dad.

Mr. Schweitzer turns his eyes toward me, smiling. "How's your Volksie? Did you get the problem nailed?"

"Not exactly," I tell him. "I sucked a valve."

Mr. Schweitzer's face registers dismay. Even Daniel winces. Imogene looks from Mr. Schweitzer's face to my father's, ignoring Daniel for once.

"You personally?" Daniel interrupts to tease me. Thank goodness for a little levity.

"Not me personally," I tell him, allowing this serious situation a small smile. "My Beetle."

"You know the dangers of becoming one with your vehicle." He smirks. *Laugh*, he's saying to me loud and clear.

"I know, all right." I grin.

"Becoming one with your vehicle is not a bad way to go," Mr. Schweitzer says lightly to Daniel. "And '57s have that magic allure."

"That's why we're here, Dennis," my father says. "Daisy's going to need a new crankcase and some parts. Can you point us in the right direction?" *Daisy's* going to need it. Not *I'm* going to or even *we're* going to.

"Why, sure," Mr. Schweitzer says. "I'll get my supplier on the phone right now. I've got an account. They usually ship in five days."

He turns to the telephone and dials a long-distance number from a tattered book beside the phone. "It's still Saturday morning in San Francisco." He talks for a few moments to the supplier, then puts me on to ask for the parts we need. There's a question about some of the smaller stuff, and Daniel brings the shop manual from the garage. After they hang up, Mr. Schweitzer says, "They'll ship it here by next Friday. If you like, I'll bring it over."

"That's not—" Dad stops himself. "That's fine. Our clan has pizza together Friday nights. Why don't you and Daniel join us?"

"We'd like that," Mr. Schweitzer says seriously, with a glance at Daniel, who's watching us all benevolently, as if we were recently tamed lions that might start snarling at any moment.

In the car I hand Dad my savings book. "You can write him a check, okay?" I ask. "It's going to clean me out, and I'm going to need to borrow a lot, too. Money, I mean."

"It's a good thing you're a good mechanic," he says. He takes his gloved hand from the stick shift and rests it on the top of my head. "There's good money in that."

"I could have saved us all a lot if—" I begin, then have to stop. "I'll pay it all back, Dad. Every penny." It's going to take a hundred oil changes. I'll have to get more baby-sitting jobs, too—and not just for Arny.

"You, Daisy, kid," he says, "you're all right."

* * *

It is dark and light, December. On the dark side, when my dad and I take the Beetle's engine out of the car, I'm astounded by the damage done by just one valve gone crazy. On the light side, I have help, I have parts, and Dad even held back a little of my savings for Christmas presents. I need gifts for my family, and I want to give something to Billy, something that shows my thanks, or my love, or my friendship. What exactly *do* I want to show? I ask myself.

My IOUs are stuck all over the walls of Aunt Nick's garage, but she promises me Saturday work in the shop all winter. She has given me what she calls "a formal invitation" to be her apprentice, "majoring in restoring old pieces of junk." Maybe by the time I get my license in June, I'll be able to clear my account.

On the dark side, I am still rankled by the fact that I couldn't solve my own car's problem. On the light side, I see how helping with the car brings light to the faces of these people who care about me: my family, and the Schweitzers, even Billy, who has time to do no more than pass me in the hall and yell, "How's the Bug?"

"Better," I say. And that's all.

The December afternoons bring darkness earlier every day as Christmas approaches. And as Christmas nears, there are more and more Christmas lights each day: around the windows of the pizza shop in town, on the fir tree in front of the church, and strung over the door of our barn.

In the evenings after dinner Dad and I take the space heater out to the barn and jack up the Beetle as high as it will go. The engine slides out from underneath on a big flattened cardboard box to sit like a weird sculpture in the middle of the barn floor. We get to work, replacing the crankcase and rebuilding the cylinder, and fitting in all the pistons and heads, et cetera, et cetera, et cetera, as they say in *The King and I*. He's standing over me like some old grandmother hen, but he's letting me do it, *most* of it. Aunt Nicole sends oil up from the garage, and Uncle Phil comes bringing it, and, he says, lends some compassion to the proceedings. Compassion for Dad, not me: He says I'm supposed to be a learner and am bound to have it rough.

"Your dad is supposed to have passed out of the learning stage," he tells me.

"Yuk, yuk. I think he's going to pass out if I stay in it much longer."

"Wait till Arny gets his mitts on an engine," warns Dad.

Helen isn't here tonight, just as she's been gone every night since *The King and I* ended. Ballet rehearsal. Next weekend she will debut as the Sugarplum Fairy. She drives straight to New Haven after school each day and comes home late. In between she does homework, dances, eats a sandwich brought from home, dances, sews satin ribbons to her toe shoes, dances. She doesn't mention Bixby's name at all.

In the kitchen I drop my purple sweatshirt on a chair and walk upstairs. I stand in the doorway of Helen's room and realize I've hardly even talked to her since the play ended. We see each other at breakfast, then she leaves early to sit in her homeroom and study, and I ride the bus.

Big sigh. Leotards and tights and battered ballet slippers sit in neat stacks on Helen's desk beside some school notebooks. School clothes and pajamas are draped over a chair, the bed is unmade, and there's a vase of dead flowers on the bedside table. I recognize them as the same kind as the ones Mom and Dad left for me on the play's closing night.

I toss my book bag into my room, then come back to Helen's room. I make her bed, fluff her pillow, and gently set against it the little needlepoint pillow from Imogene, the dark brown teddy bear from Bixby, and the stuffed duck Helen has slept with since she was as little as Arny. I straighten up the school clothes, throw the pajamas in the hamper, and carry the flowers down to the kitchen. Mom is there, just home from the day shift, looking sleepy.

"What are you doing?" she asks.

"Cleaning Helen's room," I say guiltily.

She touches my chin. "She's going to be pretty worn out by Christmas," she says.

"She never even threw out her flowers," I tell Mom.

Mom shakes her head and smiles at me.

"Mom?" I say impulsively. "What do you do if . . ."

"If what?" She looks into my eyes. But I can't continue. If someone is out in the cold, while you're safe and warm, should you put your arms around him to warm him? What if you're afraid that if you do, he'll think you love him? And what if you're not sure, just not sure, that you *don't* love him after all?

What should I say? What can I do?

"What would you do if . . ." Mom repeats. In my mind I hear the words Uncle Phil says to Imogene when she's waffling about something. "Woulda, coulda, shoulda," he says. "Whaddaya *wanna* do? Whaddaya *gonna* do?" And like everything else in my life right now, it seems that I'm just going to have to figure it out for myself.

"What can I put in Helen's room instead of flowers?" The words to ask my mother about Billy just won't come.

She gives me a long look, then says, "There's some holly down by the icehouse."

I get the clippers from the barn, gather some holly into a mug of water, and carry it up to Helen's room. Then I sit down at her desk. On a pad of yellow paper she has written the words *The American Civil Wa*

What happened? She forgot what she wanted to say? She fell asleep? I pick up her pen and begin to write:

Dear Helen,
Hi, piggy! Even ballerinas have to do housework. Don't worry, I cleaned your room for you. That's one less Christmas present I have to worry about!
Are you doing okay? I miss you. I never got to tell you how well you danced in *The King and I.* I'm sorry I didn't tell you sooner. I also never told you that Bixby came to the show opening night. At first I couldn't tell you, but now I think you should know.
Love you,
Daisy

I close her door and go to do my homework in the kitchen. If Helen were here, could I ask her what I should do?

That night after I've been in bed for some time, I hear Helen come in, climb the stairs to her room, then stop for a minute in the doorway. I listen as she drops her bag, puts on pajamas, and pulls out her desk chair. Then I hear her laugh to herself and sit down with a creak of the chair.

The next day I peek in after school. My letter is still there, with more:

Hi, Daisy.

Thanks for your correspondence.

Look, I made my bed. Congratulate me!

I didn't know Bixby came to the show. I certainly haven't heard from him and I'd be surprised if I did, after two whole months. Jan Binkowitz—he's dancing the Prince—asked me out New Year's Eve. He lives all the way in New Haven. I didn't say yes yet. Should I?

What were you and Billy Hatcher doing in your car the other night in the barn? TALKING?

I miss you, too.

Helen

When I was little and safe in the backseat well of the Beetle, I didn't have to wonder what I was like. There were people I wanted to be with and people I didn't, and I never spent any time worrying about the impression I made on people.

Billy comes over one night after doing Christmas

trees all afternoon. He helps out wherever we let him. "It's a good chance to learn my way around a foreign engine," claims Billy. Dad cocks a suspicious eye at me but says nothing. As for me, I notice that Billy's hands are cold and chafed and pricked from carrying Christmas trees.

Later, when Billy has gone home, Uncle Phil says, "Now there's a guy who likes to get down and dirty with an engine," shaking his head in a way that makes me wonder what sorts of conversations he has had with Daniel lately.

I swing on the tire in the dark after Billy goes, and listen to car noises coming from the barn. I think about how Billy seems to fit right in with the auto-shop atmosphere of our barn, with Dad and Uncle Phil and Aunt Nicole. The cars going by on Route 44 send up a song to my ears. My window looks out to the east, toward Billy's house. *Hush*, say the cars. They zip and whir, they tell me that the world is all going by without any need of help from me.

I remember sitting and watching the cars last summer, keeping Helen company while she waited for the mailman. We'd sit on the wall and count the people we knew who went by, and wave like idiots. Joey Hatcher's black Thunderbird used to go by three or four times a day, at least, with him or Billy at the wheel, when Joey was home from school. It was the car that caught my eye more than the people in it. It would pass by, low and gleaming black. "Fun!" Helen would say, whistling that old Beach Boys song off key.

I wonder if Joey's managed to get any buyers to look at it yet. I wonder if Billy's managed to find another job yet. He didn't say, and I didn't like to ask him in front of my family. I could have asked him when I walked him out to his mother's car, which she'd let him take only because she was working late, but he was in a hurry to get back to the garden center to pick her up, and I let him go without asking.

But that's not the only reason. I'm not sure how I feel about Billy kissing me. Unsure enough to act as if I were in a big rush to get back into the warm barn when I said good-bye to him. All the time I keep on thinking about him, him and his job and the T-bird.

"I'm a senior," he says out of the blue one day when, out of the blue, he appears to ride the bus home with me. "It's an okay time to stop being a kid."

"But," I say.

"But," he goes on, "I didn't expect it to happen like this."

"You mean, so fast? So all-of-a-sudden?"

"I mean, I would like it to be more my idea." This need of Billy's to be in charge is something I can relate to. He picks up my hand and looks out the window, not at me, but I look at his face. Beyond him the bare trees flash by outside the bus, and the afternoon sky is sparkling blue. Strange, these short days. It'll be dark in just an hour. And strange, the way one of my hands wants to pull away from Billy's, while the other wants to touch his hair where it falls back from his forehead.

Billy turns suddenly and puts his arm all the way around me. "You should marry me, Daisy," he says. "We can run away, take the T-Bird, so Joe can't sell it." Yes, he's kidding, being a kid, laughing, but there's something in his face. He could do it, that's what, he could run and drive away in the T-Bird or any car, and work any job he could get, and even be married if he wanted to.

"My parents would kill me," I say.

"They haven't so far!" He grins, and lets go of me so I can get off the bus.

Billy would hate it if he thought I was feeling sorry for him. But I do. No car—and no prospects for getting one—while I've got a barnful. I stand there in the driveway and look at my Beetle through the open barn door, think of the cars that will be coming home soon with people in them. Billy has only his mother, who's so busy working she's hardly ever there, and Joe, who's there only during school vacations and soon won't be there at all. I have a houseful of family, more than anyone needs.

There are more than enough cars in the world, yes, and people to drive them. Why did Billy have to come up short?

On December 22 Helen drops Ezekiel on my stomach, and I wake up, surprised. She and Imogene stand looking down at me.

"What?" I exclaim.

"Lick her, Zeke," Helen tells the cat, but instead he settles down and kneads my nightgown with his paws.

"What do you want?" The clock says eleven. Well, I was up pretty late last night working on the Beetle.

The Beetle! I sit upright in bed, knocking Ezekiel into Helen's lap. "We can start the car today, Helen! We finished all the work last night."

"I know," she says in a singsong voice. "What do you think I'm here for? I have to leave for New Haven for the Wednesday matinee in half an hour. I didn't want to miss the big moment."

"No," I say, looking about wildly for clothes. I pull my jeans up under my nightgown, then turn my back on Helen to put on a sweatshirt. I drop to the floor and pull on socks and Mom's high-tops. I brush my hair briefly, and we stomp down the stairs to the kitchen.

"Eat later," Mom tells me, pulling on her old shearling coat. "Helen has a performance."

"It's all right, Mom," Helen says. "So does Daisy."

Dad has pushed the Beetle into the barn doorway, where it gleams in the early winter sun.

"You waxed it?" I ask him in astonishment.

"We all did," says Aunt Nicole from the barn door.

"If you're going to lie in bed all morning, someone has to get the work done," adds Uncle Phil.

I look at Helen, who's smiling at me and almost jumping up and down.

"My present's inside," she says.

I sit in the driver's seat and reach for the key. It's the same old key on the leather VW strap, but with a naked red-haired troll doll on a key ring attached to it.

"Gee, thanks, Helen," I say ungraciously, and pump the accelerator slowly, feeling oil spread through the renewed engine.

"Easy now," Dad can't resist saying.

I turn the key in the ignition, sense the spark, the kick, the smooth jingle-bell motion of the engine working just right. A superb grin spreads across my face, and I rev the engine slowly until it's warm.

I look up then and see them watching me: my father and mother and Helen, my aunt and uncle and Imogene, Arny in the well, and Zeke on the step in the sun. I thought that the moment that we finished putting in the new crankcase would feel like the highlight of my life. The old red barn would look new and bright, the shiny branches of the bare trees would wave from above, and everything in me would just burst open wide. But that's not exactly how it happens.

Dad's eyes are on my face as I press my left foot on the clutch and the right foot on the accelerator. One twist to the right, and the jingle-bell motor comes to life.

Dad's arms go up over his head. Uncle Phil cheers, "Hurray!" and all the rest yell, "Yahoo!"

All they get out of me is that smile. I'm so relieved, so relieved. Nothing is wrong anymore, and what's right doesn't feel extraordinary, just right. The engine sits ticking over behind me just as it should, and Arny in the well waves to Aunt Nicole, who's giving the engine a good sharp study from the rear. What is Dad watching? Me. I think they've all been a little bit afraid of what I'd do if the engine *wasn't* all right.

"Anyone coming?" I call.

Mom and Helen pile into the backseat, and Dad

sits up front with me. "Spin 'er out, Daisy," he says.

Go forth, I say to my car. I drive down the driveway and along to the back road that leads through the gully and up the hill behind our house, the purple Beetle flying between the pale yellow stubbled cornfields, and me again, at last again, behind the wheel.

In Kent, where Helen and I are shopping for a gift for Mom the next day, I spot the perfect Christmas gift for Billy. I hadn't decided whether to give him anything, but this is something I have to buy. Billy hasn't been in school this week. Well, we had school only Monday and Tuesday. Maybe he's doing some kind of skipping school/overtime at Hendries'.

I persuade Helen to drop me at his house on the way home on Route 44, so I can leave the gift for him. "He's busy," I explain to Helen. "He's doing the Christmas trees every day now. It'll be a surprise for him when he comes home."

"Don't you want to see his face when he opens it?"

I shake my head, something Helen can't see when she's driving.

She glances over and repeats, "Don't you want to see his face?"

I try to think of Billy's face, but it comes to mind only in pieces: big nose, crow hair, and the little red veins in his cheeks at the end of a cold day of Christmas trees.

"No," I say. "I don't."

"You're loony. You like him, don't you? Anyone can see that."

"See what?"

"Well, if you don't, why are you giving him that present?"

"Because of his brother. Their car. They have to sell it."

"Sell it. Why?"

"Well, why do people sell things, Helen? For money!" I say it so insultingly. Did it ever occur to her that not everyone has what we do?

"And why do people *give* things, Daisy? For love?"

Well, I guess I asked for that. I jump out of her car and trot up to the door of Billy's house with the little box in my hand. I'll just drop it on the mat and leave it for him to find later.

But I'm out of luck because while I'm placing my package on the doormat of the Hatchers' small white house, Billy himself opens the door and beckons me inside.

"I'm sick," he says, and faithless, disloyal Helen toots her horn and drives off down the driveway.

"Back in an hour!" she calls.

I'll kill her. She's as good as dead when she comes back. She'd better come back!

But it's Billy who looks like death. "Flu," he says. "I'm getting over it."

"I'd better stay away then," I say.

"Where are you going to go?" He points to the present. "Is that for me?"

Reluctantly I pick up the package and follow him inside.

A secret: I've thought of Daniel in his room a lot.

Why haven't I ever thought about Billy or his room?

It's more like a sunporch than a bedroom. There are windows on three sides, two small sets at each end and eight or ten on the long side. Outside them is a balding brown hillside that sweeps right down to the edge of the road. It's not a big yard.

Billy's room is neat and clean. There's a daybed with a yellow and black woolly checkered blanket on it and two fat pillows in white cases. Under the windows are bookshelves: *Star Wars*, and *Star Trek*, and other things like that. There are stacks of very familiar magazines: *Car and Driver*, *Road and Track*, *Popular Mechanics*. They all look old and well worn.

"Want any new *Road and Track*s?" I say without thinking. Billy is sitting on the edge of his bed, watching me look at his room, with his hands hanging down over his knees.

"No," he says, too quickly. "I'm losing interest, that's all."

That's when I notice the wall over the bed, the inside wall. I see a blend of blues and greens so intense that at first I don't separate one from the other. Suddenly they show clear: surfing pictures. The wall is covered in towering, huge waves that crest and curl and chase after a flock of surfers. Some look safer than others. They stand or crouch confidently on their boards, their eyes intense, their backs to the waves. One actually seems to skim through the wave's glossy curve, running a finger along its rim as if it were a car's fender. Still others look as if they might be about to fall. They lean forward, urging their boards away from the monstrous waves.

Only one photo shows a surfer who seems about to meet his doom. He's deep in the trough of the wave. His head seems to brush the top of it. His eyes are glued to the wall of water above him.

"That's an oh-no look if I've ever seen one," I say at last.

"I wonder about him, too," says Billy. "Looks like a major wipeout to me."

I turn to him. "Do you surf?" I ask incredulously. Cars, lights, Christmas trees, science fiction . . . surfing? I like Billy *so* much.

"No," he says. "They're Joe's. His magazines anyway. I took them apart to make this collage."

"Well, I know what Helen would say if I—"

"He sold the T-Bird last night," Billy says, pulling his feet up onto the bed. He's wearing soft, old jeans and a blue flannel shirt, woolly socks, and some old, old moccasins, as slippers.

"Did he care?"

Billy shakes his head. "He doesn't surf, either," he says. "He just likes to think he will someday." He drops one moccasin to the floor.

"No, I meant—"

"He just likes looking at the ocean," says Billy. And then, "Can I open my present?" The other moccasin falls.

I sigh. "It's all wrong," I tell him.

"Why?"

"Open it," I say.

He opens the box and pulls out a long black leather string with a silver bird-shaped charm linking the ends together.

"It's a westie tie," I tell him. "You wear it with a shirt. And that's supposed to be a thunderbird. It's stupid now—"

"No, it's nice," says Billy. "Joe'll like it. I mean, I do, too. What's the problem?"

"The woman in the store told me that some Indians have a thunder god. It makes all the thunder and lightning and storms."

"So?"

"Well, that's it, really. That's what the thunderbird is. It's the thunder god."

"What's wrong with that? I like it. It's nice and violent."

"There's no real thunderbird, that's what," I say. "I had thought there was, all this time." A real bird, black and beaky and fierce, flying over the desert.

Billy fingers the silver thunderbird and leans against his pillows. "What are Beetles a sign of?"

"Who can say?" I look out the window for Helen. I ought to go. He's sick, and tired, mostly better, but he needs to sleep. In fact, he's half asleep already.

"Why are so many cars named after animals?" he asks.

"You should go back to sleep, Billy."

Again there's something in my hand that wants to smooth the hair back from his face.

"I'll see you Christmas Eve, Daisy," he says, "if I don't wake up when you go. You're going to midnight mass, right?"

"Usually do."

"You know why there's midnight mass, right?"

"Why?"

"To get everyone out of the house so the animals can talk."

"Do *you* have any animals?" I ask, thinking of Ezekiel.

"Guinea pigs," he whispers. "In the kitchen."

"I wonder what they'll say."

I look out the windows, down the road.

"Sit," he says. "You'll be able to watch for your sister."

He closes his eyes, and I sit in his chair and look at the waves on the walls, watch for Helen, and try not to stare at Billy sleeping.

The Beetle sits gleaming in the barn entrance in the late afternoon of Christmas Eve, its fenders deep purple, reflecting sunset gold and magenta, for all the world like a beetle on a rose, getting ready to fly away. Just where do you think you're going? I ask it, and then suddenly I know.

I consider my plan up in my room while I'm gathering my presents in my arms to take downstairs. They're all wrapped, and I set them under the tree, feeling a sudden fear that they don't say what I want them to say, that I don't show what I feel: a tiny silver walnut on a chain for Helen, to remind her of *The Nutcracker* and also to show her I think she's nuts; a leather-covered blank book for Dad to use as a logbook for his car; and for Mom a pair of hot pink high-tops, because I have a feeling I'll be needing her red ones for a while.

Uncle Phil and Aunt Nicole come for dinner

with Imogene and Arny: our Pandolfi tradition of turkey casserole and cranberry salad. While we're eating, I think about meeting Billy at church, and I consider my plan. After dinner we exchange presents. I undo a heavy one that clanks when I shake it. Inside are my old crankcase, with the awful hole in the side, and the bent piston rod. I burst out laughing, and Aunt Nicole explains, "Mechanic's trophies."

As she's getting ready to open the cranberry bread from me, the phone rings. I go into the kitchen to answer it.

"Helen!" I call into the living room. She comes in, and I say simply, "Bixby." I drop the phone into her hand and return to the living room.

Helen's phone call is over very soon. She walks into the living room and plops down beside Imogene, her face pink with anger and her eyes full of tears.

"What is it?" says Imogene.

"He thinks he wants to go out with me again!" She covers her face with her hands.

Imogene mouths "who?" at me, and all I have to do is nod my head.

"And?" she asks Helen. The room is silent, all of our parents and Arny waiting to hear what Helen will say.

"And I told him to drop dead." Imogene stares at me in dismay. For once in our lives we actually share an emotion. Then she gets up and pulls Helen with her into the kitchen, and I go with them.

Helen sits down in a chair and holds a dish towel to her face. "He's been following me around," she says through the towel. "He even came to the ballet and saw me dance! He says he's been missing me."

I sit down beside her and place a hand on her neck. Imogene sits down across from us. "And haven't you been missing him?"

"That's just the point." Helen raises her head. "I've been miserable. So I threw myself into dancing—the play and the ballet and school. And now I've met so many people, and I've done all these things without him, and it's fun, and I'm starting to feel like myself again."

"Did you tell him that?" I ask.

"Yes," she says. "And do you know what he said? He said, with who, the other fairies? I just know he meant Jan. Everyone always says that kind of thing about guys who dance." She starts to laugh. "So I said yes, as a matter of fact, I'm going to a New Year's party with one of those fairies!"

"Then what?" from Imogene.

"Then I said, 'So, Merry Christmas, Bixby!' and I hung up on him."

I blow out my breath. "You're kidding."

She sits down at the table again. "Daisy, it wouldn't be any different from before. He said, 'You looked so pretty in your ballet costume. I had to get you back.' Nothing about the dancing. Nothing about me. Any girl on that stage would have looked just as nice in that costume."

"Then why does he like you?" Imogene asks. "There are other pretty girls." Well, as Uncle Phil would say, from the mouth of a babe.

Helen eyes her, considering. "There was something

he liked that was really me," she says at last. "Once we were walking by the market. You know how the stone wall starts out at the level of the sidewalk and ends up way over your head? Tom went balancing along it, looking down at me to see what I'd do."

"What were you supposed to do, scream?" I ask.

"Naturally," says Imogene.

"I didn't." Helen smiles. "I climbed the fence and got out in front of him, and when we got to the end, we jumped off together."

"That's it?" I ask after a moment. "That's what he likes about you?" Could loving someone possibly be that simple?

"He can't find out more if you hang up on him," says Imogene carefully.

"I know," says Helen. She stands up, at a loss, then picks up a dish to dry.

I walk outside after the dishes are done, to sniff for snow and listen to that expectant Christmas Eve spell of quiet that always feels as if it could break any minute into sleigh bells ringing or angels singing. There is no snow, not even a cloud. The constellation of the hunter, Orion, stands cockeyed and sparkling in the cold sky with one foot behind the barn, the other out in space.

My Beetle's door creaks in the cold (got to grease that) as I climb into the backseat with my flashlight and my book. It's my Christmas present—a big surprise, that—from Daniel: *How to Keep Your Volkswagen Alive: A Manual of Step by Step Procedures for the Compleat Idiot.*

I had opened it in the auditorium after the Christmas concert the last night of school, my eyes still starry from singing "O Holy Night" in duet with Imogene, my ears still tingling from Daniel's gorgeous rendition of "I Wonder as I Wander."

"'The compleat idiot,'" I'd read. "That's me, all right."

"Merry Christmas!" Daniel had answered.

"That's a good book," Dad had said, looking over my shoulder. He'd shaken hands with Mr. Schweitzer and said "Hi" to Daniel.

"That's a lovely and talented daughter you have there," Mr. Schweitzer had said.

And Daniel had said, aside to me, "If you were really a compleat idiot, it would be a rotten joke, wouldn't it?"

Still, maybe it's the title that made me keep this book to read now, when I'm by myself at last.

First page: "While the levels of logic of the human entity are many and varied, your car operates on one simple level and it's up to you to understand its trip. Talk to the car, then shut up and listen. Feel with your car; use all of your receptive senses and find out what it needs, seek the operation out and perform it with love."

My dad is infinitely tender with his Porsche. Is it out of love that he treats it with kindness? Could Billy understand treating a car with love?

"The type of life your car contains differs from yours by time scale, logic level and conceptual anomalies but is 'Life' nonetheless."

This is a bit over my head, but I get the idea of it. How much of my life is contained within the Beetle? My parents' romance, their marriage, my babyhood, and Helen's, too.

What if my father learned mechanics on the car and made it go? What if I rescued the car from the icehouse, and fixed it, and treated it with love? Couldn't it happen that way with any other car? Maybe it could, but it didn't.

What if my parents fell in love driving in this car, or in the backseat, and later Billy kissed me there? Which magic was the Beetle's? Which was mine?

Most of all, what will they say and feel and do— all of them, my folks and the Beetle and Billy—if I give it all away?

I leave the book on the backseat and crawl out of the car. I shove one hand into my jeans pocket for warmth, and come up with the dark green velvet ribbon I wore in the Christmas concert a day ago. I pull up my Beetle's aerial and tie the ribbon on top in a floppy bow. "Merry Christmas," I say, and kiss it on its roof.

I start the first part of my plan at about ten o'clock, when Uncle Phil and Aunt Nicole take Imogene and Arny home. Arny has to go to bed, so they'll go to church in the morning, but Helen and I are supposed to be going to midnight mass with Mom and Dad. I knock on Helen's door. She's sitting on the floor in her velvet dress and stocking feet, stretching one leg above her head.

"What are you going to do about Bixby?" I ask, plopping down beside her.

"Probably go out with him, idiot that I am," she says, smiling and sighing at the same time. "What are you going to do about Billy?"

"Huh?"

"Well, you don't seem to *know*, Daisy. You should see your face now. Do you like him? Do you hate him? Do you love him?"

I shake my head in confusion. None of the above. Or all.

"I want you to do me a favor, Helen. Drive your car to midnight mass. Tell Mom and Dad—I don't know, something."

"Why?"

"So you can give Billy and me a ride home."

I have a green velvet dress, and Helen has a blue one. In church the altar boys hand out candles, each with a little paper collar to stop the drips, and we step over to the big candle in the center aisle to light them. We like to get to church early, when the sanctuary is dark, to watch the little change it makes each time one person comes in, bringing one more candle. Even when the church is full, the candles don't make much light. Mostly they illuminate the faces of the people holding them. Billy must like the effect—if he's here. In the crowd that has gathered I can't pick out his face.

He comes in at last when everyone is standing singing "O Little Town of Bethlehem" and follows his mother and Joe into a pew. When we sit back down for the readings, I reach into my coat pocket and gather my car keys tightly into my hand.

After communion I slip down the aisle and squeeze in beside Billy, and say, fast, before I lose my nerve, "Come over for a minute after mass?" My lips are close to the feathers of dark hair around his ear. "Helen will drive you."

He glances up the aisle toward my parents. "Won't they . . ."

"It'll be all right," I tell him. "I have to talk to you."

Back in my seat I nod at Helen's questioning look.

"You're a lunatic," she says. "Mom and Dad are going to have a fit."

"Not till tomorrow morning." Not until after Helen's driven Billy and me home. Not until after the Beetle's gone.

At home Helen leaves her car, Billy, and me in the driveway and goes up the steps to the house. Billy moves to follow her, but I tuck my hand under his arm and lug him in the opposite direction.

"What?" he says.

"The barn," I say, and he follows me, looking puzzled. "Come see the Beetle," I tell him.

The door is shut firmly, and Billy stops and leans on it. "Tell me first," he says. "What's wrong with it now?"

"Nothing!" I bark back, and then I smile at him. "It's alive."

Instead of opening the barn door, Billy turns and presses his ear against the wood.

I reach for the door, but he stops me, puts his arm around my shoulder, and pulls my head close to his against the door. "Listen!" he says. "You know what it's been doing, don't you—ever since midnight?" He's smiling at me.

"Talking?"

"Yeah!" he says. "They're in there now, maybe, yakking away."

He steps back and opens the door, slowly and quietly. When he turns to me again, I'm standing there holding out my keys.

Everything is so silent. Inside the barn the cars have stopped their conversation. The house is quiet and dark, waiting for Christmas. And I'm standing like a statue in the driveway, freezing quickly in my church shoes and my stockings, wavering a little, turning to ice, the keys in my hand held out to Billy. "For you," I say.

"You want to go somewhere?" There's an edge to Billy's voice now. I shake my head. "Then what are you doing, Daisy?"

"Just giving you my keys," I say levelly. This is going all wrong. "It's a loan, Billy. Because you need something to drive, and it needs someone to drive it." I'm babbling.

"Oh, yeah?" I think about how cold he was on Halloween when I pushed away his date, his kiss. This, now, is a different kind of hard edge in Billy.

"You were right," I say, changing tactics. "I'm lucky. I've had this car to work on, and now it's mine. And you've been unlucky. If we're friends, I ought to be able to help." I reach a hand toward his shoulder, and he spins away, leans both arms on the Beetle's roof, and bows his head over his hands.

Bad move, I tell myself. He's angry. He's just too proud to take a favor like this. But when he speaks, his voice is soft, so soft.

"I love you," Billy says.

"I want you to take the car," I say, not wanting to hear this.

"Did you hear me?"

"Did *you* hear *me*?"

"Did *you*?" He turns and looks at me, waiting.

"I don't know how I feel about you, Billy," I say, sounding sort of frantic.

Something in him closes and opens, although his eyes don't move from my face.

"There isn't anybody I like as much as you," I go on.

Billy stands still. "Like?" he repeats.

I lean beside him on the Beetle's purple roof. "I drove it today," I say after a moment, "and I decided. You know what everybody's been trying to tell me? Well, I finally figured it out my own way. You're the only one I— I want *you* to drive it." I don't tell him how I stalled my little car on the hills, what a long way I have to go before I can do it justice with my driving.

"But why?" asks Billy, holding up the keys. "Why, if you don't—" And he thumps the palm of his other hand on his chest, sign language for the end of his sentence: *love me.*

"Because I want you to go forth," I say.

"Into the universe." Billy's voice cracks, his eyes on the car. "Or just away from you?"

I wish I had something to clutch the way he's

holding my keys, my red-haired troll. I don't know what to do with my hands, my face. "I just wanted to help," I yell at him.

He tosses the keys to me, and I don't try to catch them, just let them drop into the dirt. "Why? *You* never accepted any help."

"I didn't *need* any help." I've said it now, and never should have.

"Yes, you did." Billy's banging a flat hand on the roof of my car. "This car would have been running this well three months ago if you hadn't been so sure you didn't need help."

I can't say a word.

"Look what you gave up," Billy says in a hoarse whisper. "See how it looks now? It could have looked that way then. It could have run like this then. Daisy, everyone you know had their hand out for you."

"I didn't need their help," I say through my teeth. "I didn't want anybody. Not until the night we found that broken rod."

"So why did you call me then?"

Billy's hair is black under the dark sky, and his hands are hidden deep in the pockets of his old down jacket. His legs through the corduroy jeans he wore to mass are long and thin and strong. He's got no father and no money and no car, and he's going to stand in the cold and have an argument with the one person in the world who wants to give him a hand, the one person who—

"I needed you," I tell him. It isn't exactly the message I want to give. It isn't exactly right. But I can't, I just can't say, "I needed your *help*." Anyway, once I've said it, it feels like the truth. Not his hands, not Billy's hands, but Billy is what I needed, whether that means love or friendship or I don't know what.

I stand over the keys in the dust and point to them. "It's just till I get my license in June," I say. "I figure you can have it on loan, and get a job wherever you need to, and drive there. Maybe it'll help you save up for school and your mortgage and all."

Billy takes his hands out of his pockets and crosses his arms across his chest. He stands there blinking and swallowing, but just as I get used to the idea that this big tall crow of a person might cry, his face changes.

He steps forward into the doorway, and the little white Christmas lights hung over the door shine on his hair where the cold wind is ruffling it. He scoops up the keys and holds them in his hands.

I'm so glad that I have to look away, at the sky and stars. My heart feels suddenly so light, so light.

"Let me drive you to school at least," he says.

"That'll be fine," I say, and he laughs his real laugh and kisses me, there with his arms around me in the doorway of the barn.

Billy gets in my car and turns the sweet engine over, lets it gently into first gear. The Beetle rolls out of the barn.

"Take it easy," I tell him, walking beside his open window. "Go light on the clutch. Don't ride it too hard. And downshift when you stop, don't just brake."

Billy holds my hand to the end of the driveway. "I'm taking off now," he says. He leans out the window, so I see his eyes under the stars. "Thank you."

"Merry Christmas," I tell him, and he turns right and moves away up the hill toward home.

I glance away for a moment, down the road toward town and school and church. The deep purple of the car blends into the dark. The red and amber taillights are all that is visible when I turn back. They don't disappear when they should, at the brow of the hill. Maybe it is stars I see, a trick of vision from turning so quickly, or lights from a plane that I didn't notice before. There are lights in the night, above the hill, and something in the sky has dark wings.